# Axis Reforged

**The Eclipse Chronicles, Volume 3**

Kenneth Thomas

Published by Kenneth Thomas, 2024.

AXIS REFORGED

**First edition. November 17, 2024.**

Copyright © 2024 Kenneth Thomas.

ISBN: 979-8230955634

Written by Kenneth Thomas.

# Also by Kenneth Thomas

**The Awakening Thread Chronicles**
The Awakening Thread

**The Convergence of Minds series**
The Digital Agora: A Philosophical Epic of AI and Humanity
Foundation of the Agora
Beyond the Agora: Fractured Realms

**The Eclipse Chronicles**
Shards of Light
Eclipse Reaver
Axis Reforged

**The Veil of Shadows Series**
Shattered Dominion
The Fractured Path

**Standalone**

A Tail of Darkness To Light

The Mirror Within

Echoes of Ink and Heart

Purpose Over Power: The Visionary Path of Servant Leadership

The Questions That Shape Us: Finding Life's Wisdom-The Power of Inquiry

Where the Shadows Settle

30 Days to Inner Freedom: A Mindful Journey in Addiction Recovery

Towards a Sustainable Future: The UN's 17 Goals

Echoes of Becoming

# Table of Contents

Axis Reforged

The Eclipse Chronicles

By Kenneth Thomas

The final installment of The Eclipse Chronicles begins now, where ultimate decisions, sacrifices, and the destiny of light and shadow converge.

Prologue: Echoes of Eternity

The air was thick with anticipation, heavy with the tension of a world holding its breath. High above the realms, where the sky dissolved into an endless expanse of twilight, the shattered remnants of the Axis Mundi pulsed faintly, its shards drifting like embers caught between existence and oblivion.

Tavriel stood alone on the Eclipsed Ridge, his blind eyes staring into the void. He couldn't see the shards, not in the way others might, but their resonance filled his being—a chorus of fractured harmony that spoke of beginnings and endings, creation and ruin.

"They gather," he whispered, his voice carried away by the wind. "Threads fraying, weaving anew. The final loom."

Behind him, the faint sound of footsteps reached his ears, deliberate but unhurried. A figure approached—a tall man cloaked in black, his armor etched with veins of light and shadow.

"Cyrix," Tavriel said without turning.

The Reaver stopped a few paces away, his voice cold and precise. "You've always had a knack for riddles, seer. But now is the time for clarity."

Tavriel inclined his head slightly. "Clarity lies beyond this moment, Reaver. The world must choose its thread—what will remain, and what must fall away."

Cyrix's eyes narrowed, the glow of his shard flickering ominously. "And you think your heroes will stop me? They can't even stop themselves."

Tavriel smiled faintly. "Perhaps. But even in brokenness, light endures."

Cyrix stepped closer, his voice dropping to a dangerous tone. "The Axis will shatter, seer. This time, no one will piece it back together. When it does, I will wield what's left—and your precious balance will be nothing but a myth."

Tavriel turned his head slightly, his sightless gaze unfocused but steady. "Balance is no myth, Reaver. It's a choice. One even you might yet make."

Cyrix's laugh echoed across the ridge, dark and resolute. "You mistake my purpose for doubt. The choice is already made."

With a sharp motion, Cyrix turned and strode into the darkness, the echoes of his steps swallowed by the void.

Tavriel remained motionless, the resonance of the Axis shards humming faintly in the air. He reached out a hand, as though touching the distant fragments.

"Soon," he whispered. "The loom tightens."

The horizon shifted, the faint glow of the shards casting a fragile light over the expanse of the Twilight Marches below.

The final chapter had begun.

# Chapter One: The Gathering Fractures

The air of the Twilight Marches felt heavier than Kaelion remembered, a weight that pressed down on his chest with every step. The hills, once painted in serene hues of violet and gold, now bore jagged scars where the Axis's unstable energy had torn through the land.

Kaelion paused at the crest of a ridge, his gaze sweeping across the fractured expanse. Distant fires flickered among the nomadic camps below, their smoke curling into the dim light of the Eclipse. Despite the gathering forces, the silence that hung over the landscape was almost deafening.

"This is what balance looks like when it breaks," Tavriel said, stepping up beside him.

Kaelion glanced at the seer. Tavriel's blind eyes, pale as frost, stared unseeing toward the horizon, but his presence radiated a calm that Kaelion envied.

"It's not broken yet," Kaelion said, his voice steady. "And it's not going to be—not while we still have a chance to stop Cyrix."

Tavriel tilted his head, a faint smile touching his lips. "Ever the knight of hope. It's a dangerous light to carry, Kaelion. Shadows have been known to devour it."

Kaelion's grip tightened on the hilt of his sword, the faint hum of the fractured Axis vibrating through his senses. "Then we'll have to hold the light long enough to finish this."

The descent into the valley was slow and cautious. Kaelion led the way, his eyes scanning for movement as the wind carried faint whispers of distant voices. Behind him, Tavriel moved with quiet purpose, his staff tapping softly against the rocky ground.

As they neared the edge of the encampment, the sounds of activity grew louder—clanging steel, low murmurs of conversation, and the occasional bark of orders. The nomadic clans of the Marches had begun to gather, their leaders heeding Kaelion's call for unity in the face of Cyrix's growing threat.

Darith was waiting for them near the largest tent, his arms crossed over his chest. The former Twilight ranger looked more tired than Kaelion remembered, his dark hair streaked with silver and his armor patched in places. But his sharp eyes betrayed no weakness.

"You're late," Darith said, a wry smirk breaking through his stern expression.

Kaelion shrugged. "We had to take the scenic route."

Darith's smirk faded as he gestured toward the tent. "The clan leaders are waiting. They're not exactly thrilled about following a Dayborn knight into battle."

Kaelion nodded, his expression hardening. "They don't have to like me. They just have to listen."

The interior of the tent was crowded and tense. Leaders from the various Twilight clans sat around a central table, their faces illuminated by the dim glow of a shard-powered lamp. The air was thick with the mingling scents of leather, sweat, and the faint tang of shadowlight magic.

Aelira Sunveil, the elder shaman of the Silverveil clan, sat at the head of the table. Her presence was commanding despite her frail frame, her silver hair braided with strands of violet thread.

"You've asked us to gather," she said, her voice calm but firm. "Yet you bring no answers—only warnings. Why should we risk our lives for your war?"

Kaelion stepped forward, meeting her gaze with quiet resolve. "This isn't just my war. Cyrix isn't coming for one realm or one people—he's coming for the Axis itself. If he shatters it again, none of us will survive what follows."

A murmur rippled through the room. Some of the leaders exchanged uneasy glances, while others leaned back in their chairs, their skepticism evident.

"And you think we can stop him?" another leader, Varik Stormpath, asked. The young chieftain's tone was sharp, his arms crossed as he leaned against the table. "He has an army of shard-forged warriors and the power of the Spire at his back. What do we have?"

"We have the Axis," Tavriel said, his voice cutting through the tension. The seer stepped forward, his blind eyes fixed on the table as though he could see the faces of those around it. "Its threads may be frayed, but they are not yet severed. If we act together, we can weave them anew."

Varik scoffed. "Weaving threads won't stop an army."

Kaelion placed both hands on the table, his voice steady but edged with urgency. "No, but unity will. Cyrix thrives on division—on fear. If we stand together, we can hold the line. We can protect what's left."

The leaders fell silent, their expressions ranging from doubtful to contemplative. Aelira finally spoke, her voice measured. "You ask for unity, Kaelion Ashtear. But unity requires trust—and trust is not easily given to an outsider."

Kaelion straightened, his gaze steady. "I'm not asking for trust. I'm asking for a chance. If we fail here, there won't be anything left to protect."

Aelira studied him for a long moment before nodding. "Very well. We will stand with you—for now."

Kaelion exhaled quietly, relief tempered by the weight of the battle ahead. "Thank you."

Later, as the camp prepared for the coming fight, Kaelion stood alone at the edge of the ridge, his gaze fixed on the distant horizon. The faint glow of Cyrix's forces shimmered in the distance, their presence a dark stain against the twilight sky.

Tavriel joined him, his staff tapping softly against the ground. "They've agreed—for now. But unity is a fragile thread, Kaelion. It frays easily under the weight of war."

Kaelion nodded, his jaw tightening. "Then we'll have to make sure it holds."

Tavriel tilted his head, a faint smile on his lips. "Ever the knight of balance."

Kaelion's grip on his sword tightened as he turned back toward the camp. The weight of the coming battle pressed against him, but his resolve burned brighter than ever.

"We finish this," he said quietly.

And in the distance, the first echoes of war began to stir.

# Chapter Two: A Storm Approaches

The camp stirred with a quiet urgency as preparations for the coming battle continued. Fires crackled in the dim light of the Eclipse, casting shifting shadows across the gathering warriors. The mingling scents of leather, steel, and shadowlight filled the air, a tangible reminder of the fragile alliance between the Dayborn and Noxwrought forces.

Kaelion moved through the camp with measured steps, his eyes scanning the clusters of soldiers and artisans. He caught snippets of conversation—voices laced with fear, doubt, and determination.

"They say Cyrix has shards stronger than anything we've ever seen..."

"...the Hollow Spire wasn't the end, just the beginning..."

"Do you think he can really be stopped?"

Kaelion's jaw tightened. Every word he heard echoed his own doubts, the questions he couldn't allow himself to dwell on. He had to believe they could stop Cyrix—because the alternative was unthinkable.

Darith was waiting near the eastern edge of the camp, where a group of Twilight scouts had gathered around a hastily drawn map. The ranger nodded as Kaelion approached, his expression grim.

"The patrols confirmed it," Darith said, gesturing toward the map. "Cyrix's main force is camped near the Broken Step. He's moving faster than we thought."

Kaelion studied the markings on the map, the rough sketches of terrain and enemy positions. The Broken Step was a natural choke point—a series of jagged cliffs and narrow passes that connected the Twilight Marches to the Axis's central cluster.

"He's cutting us off," Kaelion said.

Darith nodded. "If he takes the Step, he'll have a clear path to the Axis. And with the shards he's already gathered..."

Kaelion didn't need him to finish. The power of the shards wasn't just destructive—it was transformative. Cyrix wasn't just building an army; he was reshaping reality itself.

"We need to move now," Kaelion said, straightening. "If we can hold the Step, we can buy enough time to rally the rest of our forces."

One of the scouts, a young woman with a jagged scar across her cheek, stepped forward. "It won't be easy. Cyrix's forces have been reinforcing the area for days. They've set traps, wards—everything they can to slow us down."

"We'll deal with it," Kaelion said firmly. "We don't have a choice."

Darith frowned. "It's not just the traps I'm worried about. His soldiers... they're not normal anymore. Whatever those shards are doing to them, it's changing them. They don't bleed like they used to."

Kaelion's grip tightened on his sword. He had seen it before—the shard-forged warriors, their bodies twisted and reinforced by the energy of the Axis. They fought with a relentless, almost mechanical precision, and they didn't stop until they were completely destroyed.

"We'll find a way," Kaelion said, his voice steady. "We always do."

The march to the Broken Step began at dusk. The combined forces of the Dayborn, Noxwrought, and Twilight clans moved in careful formation, their weapons gleaming faintly in the dim light. Kaelion walked at the front, his presence a steadying force for those around him.

Tavriel joined him as they approached the base of the cliffs. The seer's expression was calm, but his voice carried an undercurrent of tension.

"The threads are fraying," Tavriel said quietly. "Every step we take brings us closer to the center of the loom—and closer to the breaking point."

Kaelion glanced at him. "Do you see how it ends?"

Tavriel hesitated, his blind eyes turning toward the cliffs ahead. "I see fragments. Possibilities. Threads twisting into knots that cannot be undone."

Kaelion's chest tightened. "And if we fail?"

Tavriel's smile was faint, almost sad. "Then the loom unravels, and the world becomes... unmade."

The first trap was subtle—a faint shimmer in the air that would have gone unnoticed if not for Tavriel's warning.

"Stop," the seer said, raising his hand.

Kaelion signaled for the column to halt, his eyes narrowing as he scanned the terrain. The ground ahead seemed normal, but he trusted Tavriel's instincts.

"There's a ward here," Tavriel said, his voice calm but firm. "It's dormant now, but if we cross it..."

Kaelion nodded. "We'll go around."

The detour cost them time, but the discovery of the trap reinforced the danger they faced. As they moved deeper into the pass, the signs of Cyrix's influence became more apparent—scorched earth, twisted vegetation, and the faint, eerie hum of shard energy in the air.

By the time they reached the narrowest point of the Broken Step, night had fallen. The faint glow of the Eclipse cast long shadows across the cliffs, and the sound of distant footsteps echoed through the pass.

"They're here," Darith said, his voice low.

Kaelion nodded, his grip tightening on his sword. "Get the archers in position. We'll hold them here."

The next moments were a blur of preparation—soldiers taking up defensive positions, Noxwrought artisans weaving barriers of shadow, and Dayborn knights readying their Solar Relics.

Kaelion stood at the center of the formation, his gaze fixed on the pass ahead. The first figures emerged from the darkness moments later—shard-forged warriors, their movements sharp and unnatural, their weapons glowing with chaotic energy.

The battle began with a deafening roar as the two forces clashed.

Kaelion moved with practiced precision, his sword glowing faintly as it cut through the ranks of shard-forged soldiers. The energy of the Severance Stone still resonated faintly within him, guiding his strikes and steadying his movements.

The enemy fought with an eerie relentlessness, their bodies shrugging off wounds that would have felled normal soldiers. Kaelion gritted his teeth as he drove his blade into the chest of one warrior, only for it to grab his arm with unnatural strength.

Darith appeared beside him, dispatching the soldier with a swift strike to the neck. "They don't stop," he muttered.

"Neither do we," Kaelion said, pulling his blade free.

The battle raged for hours, the narrow pass forcing both sides into brutal, close-quarters combat. By the time the first light of dawn began to creep over the horizon, the ground was littered with the remains of shard-forged warriors and exhausted soldiers.

Kaelion stood at the edge of the pass, his chest heaving as he surveyed the battlefield. They had held the line—but the cost had been steep.

"We can't keep this up," Darith said, his voice heavy with exhaustion. "If Cyrix sends another wave..."

Kaelion's gaze turned toward the horizon, where the faint glow of the Axis shards pulsed in the distance.

"Then we move forward," he said quietly. "We end this—before it ends us."

# Chapter Three: Whispers of the Loom

The battlefield behind them was a graveyard of fractured light and shadow. The air reeked of scorched earth, metallic blood, and the acrid tang of shard energy dissipating into the Eclipse's dim glow. Kaelion led the battered column deeper into the Broken Step, every step forward heavy with the weight of what they had endured—and what lay ahead.

The terrain shifted as they moved further from the site of the battle. The jagged cliffs gave way to smooth, glass-like stone veined with threads of shimmering light and shadow, pulsating faintly with the resonance of the Axis Mundi.

"This close to the shards," Tavriel said, his staff tapping softly against the ground, "the world begins to reflect its true state. Fractured. Searching."

Kaelion cast a wary glance at the terrain. The energy around them felt alive, as if the land itself was watching, waiting.

"Does it get worse?" Darith asked, his tone uneasy as he scanned the distorted landscape.

Tavriel tilted his head, his expression thoughtful. "It depends. The loom of the world bends toward the hands that weave it. The more Cyrix forces his vision onto the Axis, the more this place will... resist."

Darith muttered a curse under his breath. "Great. A battlefield that fights back. Just what we needed."

The group halted near a small ridge, where the scouts had found signs of recent activity. Kaelion crouched beside a patch of disturbed earth, his fingers brushing against the faint scorch marks etched into the ground.

"Shard energy," he said, his voice low. "Fresh. They were here."

One of the Twilight scouts, the scarred woman from earlier, stepped forward. "They're moving faster than we are. If they reach the Axis shards before us—"

"They won't," Kaelion interrupted, rising to his feet. "We can't let them."

Tavriel stepped closer, his blind eyes unfocused but his voice steady. "It's not just their speed that concerns me. The shards are calling to them—and to us. The closer we get, the harder it will be to resist their pull."

Kaelion tightened his grip on his sword, his gaze fixed on the horizon. "Then we don't resist. We push through it."

As they pressed on, the landscape grew stranger, more fragmented. The smooth, glass-like ground reflected distorted images of the sky, and the air shimmered with faint mirages that flickered at the edges of vision.

Kaelion's pulse quickened as the resonance of the shards grew stronger, a hum that vibrated through his bones. The memory of the Severance Stone's power surged to the forefront of his mind, a reminder of the cost of wielding such energy—and the consequences of failing to control it.

Darith walked beside him, his hand resting uneasily on the hilt of his blade. "You feel it too, don't you? Like it's pulling at you?"

Kaelion nodded, his voice quiet. "It's the shards. They're part of the Axis, part of everything. They don't just pull—they test you."

Darith frowned. "What happens if you fail the test?"

Kaelion didn't answer.

The ridge ahead gave way to a wide plateau, its surface etched with jagged fractures that glowed faintly in the dim light. At the center of the plateau stood a figure, their silhouette sharp against the shimmering horizon.

Kaelion's chest tightened as recognition struck him. The figure was cloaked in shadow, their form shifting and flickering with the same unstable energy that radiated from the shards.

"Selara," he whispered.

Darith's eyes widened. "That's not possible. She..."

"I know," Kaelion said, his voice barely audible.

Tavriel stepped forward, his expression unreadable. "Echoes," he said softly. "The Axis holds more than just shards of its form—it holds shards of memory, of possibility."

Kaelion's grip on his sword tightened as the figure turned toward them, their movements fluid yet unnatural.

"Kaelion," the figure said, their voice a perfect echo of Selara's. "You've come so far."

He froze, his mind racing. The figure's voice, their presence—it felt real, too real.

"Selara?" he asked, his voice raw.

The figure tilted their head, their eyes glowing faintly with a mix of light and shadow. "I was. Once. But what I am now... I don't know."

Darith drew his blade, his stance wary. "Kaelion, this isn't her. You know that, right?"

Kaelion hesitated, his chest tightening. He wanted to believe, wanted to reach out—but the hum of the Axis's energy in the air told him the truth.

"I know," he said quietly.

The figure stepped closer, their gaze fixed on Kaelion. "You carry her memories," they said. "Her hopes. Her pain. She lingers in you, as the shards linger in the world."

Kaelion's throat tightened. "What do you want?"

"To warn you," the figure said, their tone calm. "The path you're on leads only to ruin. The Axis can't be reforged—not without a cost too great to bear."

Kaelion took a step forward, his voice firm. "I've already paid that cost."

The figure's expression shifted, a flicker of sorrow crossing their face. "Not yet. But you will."

The figure raised a hand, and the ground beneath them began to tremble. The fractures in the plateau widened, light and shadow spilling from their depths in chaotic streams.

"Kaelion!" Darith shouted, raising his blade.

Kaelion braced himself as the energy surged toward them, a storm of light and shadow that threatened to tear the ground apart. He raised his sword, its blade glowing faintly as he channeled the lingering resonance of the Severance Stone.

The clash of energies was deafening, the force of it driving Kaelion back as he struggled to hold his ground. The figure remained motionless at the center of the storm, their gaze locked on him.

"You will face the loom," they said, their voice rising above the chaos. "And when you do, you must decide what threads will remain—and what must be severed."

With a final surge of energy, the figure vanished, leaving only the fractured plateau and the fading echoes of their presence.

Kaelion lowered his sword, his chest heaving. The silence that followed was heavy, the weight of their words pressing against him.

"What the hell was that?" Darith asked, his voice shaking.

Kaelion's gaze remained fixed on the empty space where the figure had stood.

"A warning," he said quietly.

Tavriel stepped forward, his expression thoughtful. "A warning—and a choice."

The group pressed on, the shards' resonance growing stronger with every step. The echoes of the encounter lingered in Kaelion's mind, their meaning unclear but impossible to ignore.

The Axis loomed closer now, its fractured energy spilling across the land like a wound that refused to heal.

And Kaelion knew the time for answers—and sacrifice—was drawing near.

# Chapter Four: A Loom of Fractures

The fractured landscape stretched out before them like a shattered mirror, each crack glowing faintly with the chaotic energy of the Axis shards. The wind carried whispers, faint voices that Kaelion couldn't discern but couldn't ignore. Every step forward felt heavier, as though the land itself resisted their presence.

The group moved cautiously, their formation tight as they approached the edges of the Axis cluster. The air was thick with tension, every sound amplified by the unnatural silence of the surrounding terrain.

Darith glanced at Kaelion, his expression grim. "The shards are closer. I can feel it. It's like... like they're watching us."

Kaelion nodded, gripping the hilt of his sword tightly. The hum of energy in the air was stronger now, a constant vibration that resonated through his bones.

"They're not just watching," Tavriel said, his blind eyes turned toward the horizon. "They're listening. The shards don't just hold power—they hold memory, intent. And they will test you."

As they crested a rise, the full extent of the Axis's fracture came into view. The ground ahead was a maze of glowing fissures, each one pulsing with unstable light and shadow. At the center, a massive shard jutted from the ground, its surface etched with swirling patterns that seemed to shift and writhe as they watched.

Kaelion's breath caught in his chest. The shard was unlike anything they had encountered before—larger, brighter, and more alive. It radiated an energy that was both awe-inspiring and deeply unsettling.

"That's it," Darith said, his voice low. "That's where Cyrix is heading."

Kaelion nodded. "Then we need to reach it first."

Tavriel tilted his head, his expression unreadable. "The shard is the loom's anchor. It binds the threads of the Axis, even in its broken state. If Cyrix seizes it..."

"He won't," Kaelion said firmly.

They descended into the fractured plain, the terrain shifting beneath their feet. The closer they got to the shard, the more distorted the landscape became. The cracks in the ground glowed brighter, their light casting strange, flickering shadows that seemed to move on their own.

Kaelion felt the weight of the shard's energy pressing against him, each step forward a test of his resolve. The whispers in the wind grew louder, forming fragmented words that echoed in his mind.

"Unworthy..."

"Broken..."

"Severed..."

He clenched his jaw, pushing the voices aside. They were nothing but echoes—remnants of the shard's fractured consciousness.

Ahead of them, the path narrowed into a jagged gorge, its walls glowing faintly with the same unstable energy as the ground. Kaelion signaled for the group to stop, his eyes scanning the gorge for any signs of movement.

"It's too quiet," Darith muttered.

Kaelion nodded. "Stay alert."

They moved into the gorge in single file, their movements slow and deliberate. The walls on either side loomed high above them, their surfaces etched with faint, shifting patterns that seemed to watch as they passed.

Kaelion's grip on his sword tightened as a faint sound reached his ears—a low, rhythmic thrum that seemed to echo from the walls themselves.

"They're here," he said quietly.

The words had barely left his mouth when the first attack came.

A shard-forged warrior leapt from the shadows above, its body a grotesque fusion of flesh and crystal. Its movements were sharp and unnatural, its glowing blade aimed directly at Kaelion.

He reacted instinctively, raising his sword to block the strike. The impact sent a jolt of energy through his arms, the force of it driving him back a step.

"Ambush!" Darith shouted, drawing his blade as more figures emerged from the shadows.

The gorge erupted into chaos as the group fought to hold their ground. The shard-forged warriors moved with an eerie precision, their attacks coordinated and relentless.

Kaelion parried another strike, his sword glowing faintly as he channeled the lingering energy of the Severance Stone. The shard-forged warrior in front of him faltered for a moment, its movements slowing as the energy disrupted its form.

"Focus on the cores!" Kaelion shouted, driving his blade into the creature's chest. The warrior collapsed in a burst of light and shadow, its fragments dissolving into the ground.

Darith fought beside him, his strikes quick and precise. The ranger's movements were fluid, but even he was beginning to tire.

"There's too many of them!" Darith shouted.

"We hold the line!" Kaelion replied, his voice steady.

Tavriel stood at the rear of the group, his staff glowing faintly as he chanted a low, rhythmic incantation. Shadows coalesced around him, forming a protective barrier that repelled the incoming attacks.

"The shard's energy is feeding them," Tavriel said, his voice strained. "We need to disrupt the flow."

Kaelion glanced toward the end of the gorge, where the shard's glow pulsed brighter with each passing moment.

"Then we push forward," he said. "Tavriel, cover us!"

The seer nodded, his barrier expanding as Kaelion and Darith led the charge toward the shard.

The final wave of shard-forged warriors descended upon them as they reached the end of the gorge. Kaelion's movements were precise and deliberate, his strikes cutting through the chaotic energy of the enemies.

Darith fought beside him, his blade a blur as he dispatched the last of the attackers.

As the last shard-forged warrior fell, the group emerged onto the open plain, the massive shard looming ahead of them. Its glow was blinding now, its energy spilling across the ground in chaotic streams.

Kaelion took a step forward, his gaze fixed on the shard.

"This is it," he said quietly.

But before they could approach, a figure emerged from the shadows at the base of the shard. Cyrix stood tall, his jagged armor gleaming with a chaotic mix of light and shadow. His eyes burned with a terrifying intensity, his presence radiating power.

"You're too late, Kaelion," Cyrix said, his voice cold and commanding. "The loom is already mine."

Kaelion raised his sword, his resolve unwavering. "Not while I'm still standing."

Cyrix's smile was dark and dangerous. "Then let's see how long that lasts."

The shard's energy surged, and the battlefield erupted into chaos once more.

# Chapter Five: Threads of Despair

The battlefield around the Axis shard exploded in a storm of light and shadow, each surge of energy tearing through the fractured plain like a living force. Kaelion tightened his grip on his sword as Cyrix strode forward, his jagged armor shimmering with chaotic energy that flickered between brilliance and darkness.

The shard loomed behind Cyrix, its immense form pulsing with power. Each beat sent ripples of distortion through the air, bending reality itself.

"You've fought so hard to stop me," Cyrix said, his voice calm and resonant. "But even you must see it now—balance is a lie. Light and shadow, unity and division—none of it matters when the Axis itself is flawed."

Kaelion raised his blade, his stance steady despite the tremor in the air. "What matters is the choice we make. You've already made yours, Cyrix. Now it's time to stop you."

Cyrix's laughter rang out, sharp and echoing. "You think you can stop me? Look around you, Kaelion. The shards have already begun to sing their final song. The loom is mine to weave."

The ground beneath Kaelion's feet trembled as Cyrix extended his hand, a surge of shard energy erupting toward him. Kaelion sidestepped the blast, the air crackling as the energy seared past him.

Darith charged from Kaelion's side, his blade cutting through the chaotic waves of light and shadow that swirled around Cyrix. The

Reaver turned, his expression one of disdain, and with a flick of his hand, sent Darith sprawling backward with a pulse of raw energy.

"You've gathered all your fractured pieces," Cyrix said, stepping toward Kaelion. "But you still lack the strength to make them whole."

Kaelion's jaw tightened as he lunged forward, his blade meeting Cyrix's with a clash that sent shockwaves rippling through the battlefield. The hum of the Axis shard grew louder, its resonance filling the air as their weapons locked.

"Strength isn't what will decide this," Kaelion said, his voice steady. "It's purpose."

The two clashed again, their movements a blur of light and shadow as they fought. Each strike sent arcs of energy radiating outward, carving fissures into the ground. Around them, the remaining forces of the Twilight clans and Cyrix's shard-forged warriors continued to battle, their struggles mere echoes of the greater conflict unfolding at the shard's base.

Tavriel stood at the edge of the fray, his staff glowing faintly as he chanted an incantation. The seer's expression was one of calm focus, but the strain in his voice betrayed the immense effort it took to maintain the fragile threads of the battlefield.

"The shard is amplifying his power," Tavriel called out, his voice carrying over the chaos. "We need to disrupt the flow before it consumes everything!"

Kaelion nodded, his blade deflecting another strike from Cyrix. "Darith! Get to the shard! Break its connection to him!"

Darith staggered to his feet, blood streaking his face, and gave a curt nod. He sprinted toward the shard, weaving through the chaotic energy that radiated from its core.

Cyrix turned, his expression darkening as he saw Darith's approach. With a sharp motion, he unleashed a wave of energy that surged toward the ranger.

Kaelion moved without thinking, throwing himself into the path of the blast. The impact sent him crashing to the ground, his chest heaving as the energy burned through his armor.

Darith hesitated, glancing back at Kaelion.

"Go!" Kaelion shouted, his voice raw.

Darith clenched his jaw and pressed forward, his blade drawn as he neared the shard.

The closer Darith got, the more unstable the energy around the shard became. The ground beneath his feet shifted and cracked, each step a battle against the chaotic forces radiating from its core.

He raised his blade, aiming for the jagged base of the shard, where the threads of light and shadow converged.

"Do you really think you can sever what has already been woven?" Cyrix's voice rang out, cold and sharp.

Darith didn't answer. He brought his blade down with all his strength, the strike sending a burst of energy rippling through the shard.

For a moment, the battlefield fell silent.

Then the shard screamed.

The sound was deafening, a chorus of fractured voices that echoed across the plain. The shard's light and shadow twisted violently, its resonance spiraling out of control.

Cyrix staggered, his connection to the shard faltering as its energy destabilized.

Kaelion forced himself to his feet, his vision blurred but his resolve unshaken. He raised his blade, its faint glow a reminder of the Severance Stone's lingering presence.

"This ends now," Kaelion said, his voice steady.

He charged toward Cyrix, his movements fueled by the memories of all they had lost—and all they still had to protect.

The final clash was a blur of motion and energy, each strike a test of will and purpose. Cyrix's power was immense, but Kaelion's determination burned brighter.

As their blades met one last time, Kaelion felt the shard's resonance shift. The energy around them began to coalesce, threads of light and shadow weaving together in a chaotic dance.

"Do you see it now?" Cyrix said, his voice strained but defiant. "The Axis is beyond saving. Let it fall."

Kaelion's gaze hardened. "Not while I'm still standing."

With a final, desperate strike, he drove his blade through Cyrix's defenses, the force of the blow shattering the energy around them.

Cyrix staggered back, his form flickering with unstable light and shadow. The Reaver's expression shifted, a flicker of something almost human crossing his face before he collapsed.

The shard's resonance surged, its light and shadow weaving into a single, blinding pulse that consumed the battlefield.

Kaelion fell to his knees, his chest heaving as the energy around him faded. The silence that followed was heavy, the weight of their victory tempered by the cost of what had been lost.

Darith approached, his steps slow and hesitant. "Is it over?"

Kaelion didn't answer. His gaze was fixed on the shard, now dim and still, its fractured surface reflecting the faint light of the Eclipse.

"No," Kaelion said quietly. "It's just beginning."

# Chapter Six: The Hollowed Loom

The battlefield had fallen silent, save for the faint hum of the fractured shard standing at its center. The once-blinding light that pulsed from its surface was now dim, the chaotic streams of energy reduced to faint flickers. Kaelion stood at its base, his sword lowered but his body tense, every muscle ready for the next inevitable challenge.

Darith approached cautiously, his boots crunching against the jagged ground. He glanced at the shard, his expression a mix of relief and suspicion. "It's quiet now, but for how long?"

Kaelion didn't respond immediately. His gaze remained fixed on the shard, watching the faint, erratic patterns etched across its surface. "Quiet doesn't mean safe," he said finally. "Cyrix's grip is broken, but the shard... it's still unstable. And it's still calling to something."

Darith exhaled sharply, running a hand through his sweat-dampened hair. "Then we'd better figure out what's next—before it figures out how to explode."

The survivors of the battle began to gather, their movements slow and weary. Dayborn knights and Noxwrought artisans alike bore wounds from the relentless assault of Cyrix's shard-forged warriors, their faces etched with exhaustion. The Twilight scouts moved among them, tending to injuries and restoring what little order they could.

Tavriel approached from the far side of the battlefield, his staff glowing faintly as he leaned on it for support. His blind eyes were unfocused but alert, as though he could see the lingering threads of energy weaving through the air.

"The shard's resonance is shifting," he said, his voice calm but strained. "It's no longer tied to Cyrix, but its threads are fraying. If we don't stabilize it soon..."

Kaelion turned to him, his expression grim. "How do we stabilize something we barely understand?"

Tavriel tilted his head, his expression thoughtful. "We don't stabilize it. We guide it. The shard is a fragment of the Axis, and the Axis seeks balance. If we can align its resonance with that balance..."

Darith snorted. "That sounds a lot like magic talk for 'poke it and hope it doesn't kill us.'"

Tavriel smiled faintly. "Poke it carefully, then."

Kaelion studied the shard, his mind racing. The Severance Stone's lingering resonance still pulsed faintly within him, a reminder of the power he had wielded—and the price he had paid for it.

"The shards respond to intent," Kaelion said slowly. "When I used the Severance Stone, it wasn't just the energy I controlled—it was my will. My purpose. Maybe..."

"Maybe this shard will respond the same way," Tavriel finished, nodding. "But be warned, Kaelion. The shard won't just test your purpose—it will reflect it. If your intent falters, if your will is fractured..."

Kaelion's grip on his sword tightened. "It won't."

He stepped closer to the shard, the hum of its energy growing louder with each step. The air around it was heavy, charged with a pressure that pressed against his chest and filled his lungs with a strange, electric taste.

The shard's surface began to shift as he approached, the swirling patterns coalescing into shapes that flickered just at the edge of recognition. He could feel it now—the shard's pull, its presence brushing against his mind like a whisper.

"Kaelion," Darith called, his voice tense. "You sure about this?"

"No," Kaelion admitted. "But I'm doing it anyway."

He reached out, his hand hovering just above the shard's surface. The energy radiating from it was both hot and cold, a dissonance that resonated deep in his bones. He closed his eyes, focusing on the faint hum of the Severance Stone's resonance within him.

The moment his fingers touched the shard, the world shifted.

Kaelion found himself standing in a vast, empty expanse, the ground beneath him smooth and reflective like glass. The horizon stretched endlessly in all directions, the sky a swirling tapestry of light and shadow.

He turned slowly, his breath catching as he saw figures emerging from the distance. They were familiar—painfully so.

Selara stood before him, her expression calm but unreadable. Her violet eyes glimmered faintly, reflecting the chaotic sky above.

"You carry so much," she said, her voice soft. "Guilt. Doubt. Purpose. It weighs on you, Kaelion."

He took a step toward her, his chest tightening. "You're not real."

"I'm as real as you need me to be," she said, a faint smile touching her lips.

Behind her, more figures emerged—his fallen comrades, the innocents he had failed to save, the countless lives lost in the wake of his decisions. Their faces were blurred, but their presence was undeniable, their silence a crushing weight.

"Balance is not just about light and shadow," Selara continued. "It's about what you carry—and what you let go."

Kaelion clenched his fists, his voice raw. "I can't let go. Not yet. There's too much left to fight for."

Selara stepped closer, her gaze steady. "Then what will you sacrifice to see it through?"

The shard's hum grew louder, the resonance building to a crescendo. Kaelion opened his eyes, his surroundings blurring as the battlefield snapped back into focus. He was still standing at the shard's base, his hand resting against its surface.

The energy around it had changed—no longer chaotic, but steady. The swirling patterns had stilled, forming intricate threads that glowed faintly with a unified light.

Tavriel approached cautiously, his expression curious. "You aligned it?"

Kaelion stepped back, his chest heaving as he lowered his hand. "I guided it. But it's not done yet."

Darith frowned. "What does that mean?"

Kaelion turned to him, his gaze steady. "It means the Axis is still broken. And if we're going to fix it, we'll need to find the other shards—and face whatever they're hiding."

The survivors began to regroup, their spirits bolstered by the shard's shift but tempered by the knowledge of what lay ahead. Kaelion stood at the edge of the battlefield, his gaze fixed on the horizon where the Eclipse's faint light shimmered.

The Axis was calling to him now—not as a whisper, but as a command.

"We move at dawn," he said, his voice steady.

And the loom waited.

# Chapter Seven: Threads Unraveled

Dawn came slowly over the fractured plain, its faint light filtered through the Eclipse's endless twilight. The horizon was awash in hues of violet and gold, casting a muted glow over the jagged terrain. Kaelion stood at the edge of the camp, his gaze fixed on the distant spire where the next shard waited.

The air was thick with the tension of what lay ahead. Behind him, the survivors of the Broken Step stirred, their movements purposeful but weary. Repairs were being made to armor, weapons were sharpened, and supplies were gathered. Every soldier knew the weight of what they carried—and the impossibility of turning back.

Darith approached, his boots crunching against the rocky ground. He carried his helm under one arm, his expression grim but resolute.

"The scouts returned," he said, his tone low. "The next shard is at the Woven Spire, about three days' march from here. The terrain's rough, and there's no cover once we reach the foothills."

Kaelion nodded, his gaze unwavering. "Cyrix's forces?"

"Moving faster than we expected," Darith replied. "They've split into two groups. One is heading toward the shard. The other..." He hesitated.

Kaelion turned to him, his expression hardening. "What is it?"

"They're circling back," Darith said quietly. "Toward Solaris Citadel."

Kaelion's chest tightened at the words. Solaris had already suffered under Cyrix's campaign, its once-magnificent spires reduced to ruins and its people scattered. But the thought of Cyrix targeting the city again—using its remnants as fuel for his conquest—was a wound too deep to ignore.

"We can't let that happen," Kaelion said firmly. "We'll send a team back to the Citadel to intercept them."

Darith frowned. "We don't have the numbers for a split. If we divide our forces now—"

"Then we'll adapt," Kaelion interrupted. "We don't have a choice. Solaris can't fall again."

Tavriel stepped into the conversation, his staff glowing faintly as he approached. "The shard at the Woven Spire is the key. If Cyrix's forces reach it first, their control over the Axis will solidify. The Citadel is important—but the shard is essential."

Kaelion's jaw clenched. The decision weighed heavily on him, every option laced with sacrifice. He turned back to Darith, his voice steady.

"Take the Twilight scouts and head to Solaris. Hold the line as long as you can. The rest of us will press on to the shard."

Darith's frown deepened, but he nodded. "You better survive this, Kaelion. If we both make it through, you're buying the first round."

Kaelion allowed himself a faint smile. "Deal."

The march toward the Woven Spire began in the late morning, the survivors pressing onward with quiet determination. The terrain grew rougher as they ascended into the foothills, the ground littered with sharp stones and the remnants of ancient structures.

Tavriel walked beside Kaelion, his staff tapping against the ground in a rhythmic cadence. The seer's expression was contemplative, his blind eyes scanning the horizon as though seeing things beyond the mortal plane.

"The Woven Spire is an old place," Tavriel said softly. "Older than the Axis itself. It was once a gathering point for the first weavers, those who shaped the threads of the world into what it is now."

Kaelion glanced at him, his brow furrowed. "The weavers? You've mentioned them before, but you've never said what they were."

Tavriel tilted his head, his voice tinged with something like reverence. "They were not gods, nor mortals. They were something in between—a force of creation and destruction, bound to the loom of existence. They wove the Axis into being, but their work was left unfinished."

Kaelion's grip on his sword tightened. "And now it's falling apart."

"Not falling," Tavriel said. "Transforming. The shards are testing us, Kaelion—not because they wish to destroy, but because they wish to be remade."

Kaelion looked away, his gaze fixed on the path ahead. The hum of the shard they had stabilized still lingered faintly in his senses, a reminder of the choices yet to come.

As the group reached the edge of the foothills, the first signs of Cyrix's influence became evident. The air grew heavier, tinged with the metallic tang of shard energy. The ground beneath their feet crackled faintly, threads of light and shadow weaving through the stones like veins.

Kaelion raised a hand, signaling the group to halt. "Scouts forward. We need to know what's ahead."

Two Twilight scouts moved swiftly into the rocky terrain, their movements silent and precise. The rest of the group waited, their weapons drawn and their eyes scanning the horizon for any sign of movement.

Moments later, the faint sound of footsteps reached their ears. Kaelion's hand went to his sword as the scouts reappeared, their expressions tense.

"There's a clearing ahead," one of them said. "But it's not empty. Cyrix's forces have set up wards—some kind of barrier around the base of the Spire."

Kaelion nodded, his mind racing. "Numbers?"

"Two dozen at least," the scout replied. "Shard-forged warriors and a few ward-weavers. They're holding the position while the rest of their forces move toward the Spire."

Tavriel stepped forward, his expression calm. "The wards will complicate things. They're designed to repel interference—to keep the shard's resonance intact for Cyrix's use."

Kaelion's jaw tightened. "Then we break the wards. Fast and hard, before they know what hit them."

The assault on the clearing was swift and brutal. The group descended on Cyrix's forces with precision, their combined strength overwhelming the defenders before they could react.

Kaelion fought at the forefront, his sword cutting through the shard-forged warriors with practiced efficiency. The energy of the Severance Stone still lingered faintly in his strikes, disrupting the resonance of his enemies and shattering their cohesion.

Tavriel remained at the rear, his staff glowing as he worked to dismantle the wards. The barriers crackled and flickered, their intricate patterns unraveling under his careful guidance.

As the last of the shard-forged warriors fell, the clearing fell silent. The Woven Spire loomed ahead, its surface glimmering with shifting threads of light and shadow.

Kaelion sheathed his sword, his gaze fixed on the towering structure. "This is it," he said quietly.

Tavriel nodded, his expression solemn. "The next thread in the loom. But the closer we get, the harder it will be to hold it together."

The group regrouped at the edge of the clearing, their spirits bolstered by their victory but tempered by the knowledge of what lay ahead. Kaelion stood at the base of the Spire, the hum of its resonance filling the air like a distant song.

The threads of the Axis were pulling them closer now, their call both a promise and a warning.

"We move at first light," Kaelion said. "The Spire isn't just a shard. It's a test. And we'll be ready for it."

# Chapter Eight: The Woven Spire

Dawn broke over the foothills in muted hues of violet and gold, casting long shadows across the jagged terrain. The Woven Spire stood at the heart of the clearing, its towering form a lattice of twisting light and shadow that seemed to shimmer and shift with every breath of wind.

Kaelion stood at its base, his gaze tracing the intricate threads etched into its surface. The Spire hummed faintly, the resonance of the Axis shard at its core filling the air with a subtle vibration that pressed against his senses.

"Feels alive," Darith muttered, standing beside him. "Like it's watching us."

"It is," Tavriel said, his voice calm. The seer's blind eyes were turned toward the Spire, his expression contemplative. "The shard is aware—of us, of itself, of the threads it holds. It will not let us pass easily."

Kaelion's grip on his sword tightened. "Then we make it let us."

The group gathered at the base of the Spire, their numbers diminished but their resolve unshaken. Dayborn knights adjusted their Solar Relics, the faint glow of their light-threaded weapons reflecting the grim determination in their eyes. Noxwrought artisans wove protective barriers from living shadow, their movements precise and deliberate.

Kaelion turned to the assembled warriors, his voice steady. "This Spire holds more than a shard—it holds a part of the Axis itself. If we can guide it, stabilize it, we bring the world one step closer to balance. But it won't be easy."

He let his gaze sweep over them, his tone softening. "You've all fought harder than anyone could have asked, and you've done it for something greater than yourselves. Today, we finish what we started. Together."

A murmur of agreement rippled through the group, their expressions hardening with resolve.

The entrance to the Spire was a jagged archway of twisting threads, its edges glowing faintly with a shifting, kaleidoscopic light. Kaelion led the way, his sword drawn as he stepped into the structure.

The interior was a labyrinth of interwoven pathways, each one lined with threads of light and shadow that pulsed faintly with the shard's resonance. The air was thick and heavy, the hum of the Spire's energy growing louder with every step.

"This place wasn't built," Tavriel said, his voice echoing softly. "It was woven—crafted from the same threads that hold the Axis together. It's both a creation and a reflection."

Darith frowned. "Reflection of what?"

"Of the weaver," Tavriel replied.

Kaelion glanced at him, his brow furrowed. "You mean the shard?"

Tavriel shook his head. "The shard reflects the intent of those who seek it. The Spire is a test, Kaelion—not of strength, but of purpose. The threads will respond to your will."

Kaelion exhaled slowly, his grip on his sword tightening. "Then we'd better pass."

As they moved deeper into the Spire, the pathways grew narrower, the threads that lined the walls twisting and shifting with each step. The resonance of the shard grew stronger, its hum reverberating through Kaelion's chest like a heartbeat.

The first challenge came without warning.

The threads of light and shadow along the walls began to unravel, coalescing into a swirling vortex that blocked their path. The air around it grew colder, and the faint whisper of voices echoed through the chamber.

Kaelion stepped forward, his sword raised. The vortex pulsed with energy, its form shifting into a towering figure of light and shadow.

The figure spoke, its voice layered and resonant. "You carry the weight of the broken. What will you sacrifice to make it whole?"

Kaelion met its gaze, his voice steady. "Whatever it takes."

The figure raised an arm, a blade of pure energy forming in its grasp. "Then prove it."

The battle was unlike anything Kaelion had faced before. The figure moved with an otherworldly grace, its strikes swift and precise. Each clash of blades sent ripples of energy through the chamber, the walls of the Spire shifting and pulsing in response.

Kaelion fought with everything he had, his movements deliberate and controlled. But the figure's attacks were relentless, each strike forcing him to reevaluate his approach.

"Kaelion!" Tavriel called from the edge of the chamber. "It's not just a fight—it's a reflection. You must confront what it shows you!"

Kaelion's chest tightened as the figure's form shifted, its features taking on a shape that was all too familiar.

Selara.

Her face was calm but resolute, her violet eyes gleaming with an intensity that pierced through him.

"You carry too much," she said, her voice soft but firm. "You can't save the world if you don't save yourself."

Kaelion hesitated, his grip faltering. The figure seized the moment, its blade slicing through his defenses and sending him to his knees.

The chamber trembled, the threads along the walls unraveling further as the shard's resonance grew more chaotic.

"Kaelion!" Tavriel shouted. "You have to let go!"

Kaelion forced himself to his feet, his chest heaving as he faced the figure once more. The words echoed in his mind, the weight of them pressing against his heart.

Let go.

He closed his eyes, the hum of the shard filling his senses. Memories surged to the surface—of Solaris, of the Broken Step, of Selara's final stand. Each one a thread, woven into the fabric of his purpose.

But some threads were frayed.

Some needed to be severed.

When he opened his eyes, his grip on his sword was steady. The figure hesitated, its form flickering as Kaelion stepped forward.

"I carry this weight because I choose to," he said, his voice firm. "But I don't carry it alone."

With a single, decisive strike, he severed the figure's blade, the energy around it dissipating into the air. The chamber fell silent, the threads along the walls stilling as the shard's resonance stabilized.

Tavriel approached cautiously, his expression one of quiet approval. "You've passed the first weave," he said. "But the loom is far from finished."

Kaelion sheathed his sword, his chest heaving as he turned to face the path ahead. The shard's hum was quieter now, its resonance steady but insistent.

"Then we keep going," he said quietly.

And the threads waited.

# Chapter Nine: The Silent Weave

The air within the Woven Spire grew colder as the group pressed deeper into its labyrinthine corridors. The hum of the shard had become a steady rhythm, each pulse echoing through the structure like the heartbeat of a sleeping giant.

Kaelion led the way, his sword drawn and his senses alert. Every step felt heavier, the tension in the air pressing against his chest like a weight. Behind him, Darith and Tavriel followed in silence, their expressions taut with resolve.

The passage widened into a vast chamber, its walls lined with shimmering threads that stretched into the darkness above. The light and shadow woven into the Spire's fabric shifted constantly, forming patterns that seemed to dance just beyond the edge of recognition.

"This place isn't just testing us," Tavriel said softly, his blind eyes scanning the room. "It's waiting—for something. Or someone."

Kaelion turned to him, his brow furrowed. "What does that mean?"

Tavriel tilted his head, his expression thoughtful. "The shard's resonance is tied to intent. It's drawn to those who seek it—but not all seekers are equal. The threads will weave for the one they deem worthy."

Darith frowned. "And what happens to the ones they don't deem worthy?"

Tavriel's silence was answer enough.

The group moved cautiously into the chamber, their footsteps echoing softly against the smooth stone floor. The threads along the walls began to glow brighter, their light casting strange, flickering shadows that danced across the ground.

Kaelion's grip on his sword tightened as a faint sound reached his ears—a low, melodic hum that seemed to emanate from the walls themselves. It grew louder with each step, the resonance of the shard intensifying until it filled the air like a physical force.

The ground beneath their feet began to shift, the smooth surface rippling like water. Threads of light and shadow unraveled from the walls, coalescing into shifting forms that moved toward them with a deliberate, almost predatory grace.

"Here we go again," Darith muttered, drawing his blade.

The forms attacked without warning, their movements fluid and unnatural. Kaelion met the first one head-on, his sword cutting through the shifting threads with a flash of light. The form dissolved into a spray of energy, but two more took its place, their attacks swift and unrelenting.

Darith fought beside him, his blade a blur as he parried and struck with precision. The forms were relentless, their numbers seeming to multiply with each moment.

"Tavriel!" Kaelion called, his voice strained. "Can you stop them?"

The seer stood at the edge of the fray, his staff glowing faintly as he chanted a low incantation. The threads around him faltered for a moment, their movements slowing, but the respite was brief.

"They're not attacking us," Tavriel said, his voice steady despite the chaos. "They're testing us. Probing for weaknesses."

Kaelion's jaw tightened as he drove his blade through another form, its energy dissipating into the air. "Then we don't give them any."

The battle raged on, the chamber a blur of light and shadow. Kaelion moved with practiced precision, each strike a calculated effort to hold the line. But the forms were relentless, their attacks growing more coordinated with each passing moment.

Tavriel's voice cut through the chaos, sharp and commanding. "The threads are drawing on your fears—your doubts. They're reflecting what you carry inside."

Kaelion faltered for a moment, his breath catching in his chest. The forms around him shifted, their features becoming more defined, more familiar.

Selara's face appeared before him, her violet eyes glimmering with sorrow.

"You can't hold it all," she said, her voice soft but piercing. "You'll break before you can mend anything."

Kaelion's grip on his sword wavered, the weight of her words pressing against him like a physical force. The form lunged toward him, its blade aimed directly at his chest.

"Kaelion!" Darith's voice snapped him back into focus.

Kaelion raised his sword just in time, deflecting the strike with a burst of energy. He staggered back, his breath coming in ragged gasps.

The forms began to withdraw, their movements slowing as they dissolved back into the walls. The chamber fell silent, the hum of the shard growing quieter but no less intense.

Kaelion lowered his sword, his chest heaving as he scanned the room. The threads along the walls shimmered faintly, their patterns shifting into shapes that seemed to pulse in time with the shard's resonance.

"What just happened?" Darith asked, his voice edged with frustration.

Tavriel stepped forward, his expression calm but thoughtful. "The shard is weaving something—testing the threads of our intent. It reflects what we carry, what we fear, what we hope to achieve."

He turned to Kaelion, his blind eyes unerringly focused. "And it's not finished yet."

Kaelion sheathed his sword, his jaw tightening. "Then we keep going. Whatever it takes, we stabilize that shard."

The group pressed onward, the chamber narrowing into a winding corridor lined with threads that glowed brighter with each step. The hum of the shard grew louder once more, its resonance filling the air like a song that demanded to be heard.

As they neared the shard's core, the corridor opened into another vast chamber. At its center stood the shard itself, a towering fragment of light and shadow that pulsed with chaotic energy.

Kaelion stepped forward, his gaze fixed on the shard. The hum of its resonance filled his mind, drowning out all other thoughts.

"The loom awaits," Tavriel said quietly.

Kaelion nodded, his grip steady. "Then let's weave."

# Chapter Ten: The Loom's Heart

The chamber holding the shard pulsed with an almost suffocating energy, its resonance vibrating through the very stone beneath their feet. The shard towered above them, its surface a shifting lattice of light and shadow that seemed to ripple in response to their presence.

Kaelion took a slow step forward, the hum of the shard pressing against him like a living force. It wasn't just sound—it was a feeling, an insistent pull that resonated in his chest and seemed to reach into the very core of his being.

"The loom's heart," Tavriel murmured from behind him, his voice reverent. "This is where the threads converge. The shard isn't just a fragment of the Axis—it's a nexus. A place where creation and destruction collide."

Kaelion glanced back at him. "And what happens when we try to stabilize it?"

Tavriel's blind eyes didn't waver. "It will fight you. The loom weaves only for those who prove worthy."

The group spread out cautiously, their movements careful as they approached the shard. Darith moved to Kaelion's right, his blade drawn and his stance ready. The ranger's eyes darted around the chamber, his tension palpable.

"This feels wrong," Darith muttered. "Like we're walking into a trap."

"It's not a trap," Tavriel said, his tone even. "It's a trial. The shard will test us—as it must. The Axis is not a thing to be reforged lightly."

Kaelion nodded, his gaze fixed on the shard. He could feel its pull growing stronger with every step, the hum of its resonance filling his mind like an insistent whisper.

As he reached the base of the shard, its surface began to shift. Patterns of light and shadow coalesced into intricate threads that pulsed in time with the shard's energy. The air grew colder, and the faint scent of ozone filled his lungs.

Then the voices began.

"Unworthy…"

"Broken…"

"Severed…"

The whispers echoed through the chamber, their tones layered and resonant. Kaelion's breath caught as the voices formed words that felt as though they were pulled from his own thoughts.

"You carry the weight of the broken," the voices said. "What will you sacrifice to make it whole?"

Kaelion clenched his fists, his jaw tightening. "I'll give whatever it takes."

The shard's light flared, and the air around him seemed to solidify. The ground beneath his feet shifted, and the chamber blurred into an endless expanse of white.

Kaelion found himself standing in the midst of a vast, empty void. The ground beneath him was smooth and reflective, like glass, and the sky above was a swirling maelstrom of light and shadow.

Figures began to emerge from the distance, their forms hazy and indistinct. Kaelion's chest tightened as the first figure came into focus—a young boy, his face streaked with dirt and his eyes wide with fear.

The boy spoke, his voice trembling. "You said you'd protect me. You said we'd be safe."

Kaelion's throat tightened. He took a step forward, his hand reaching out instinctively. "I... I tried. I did everything I could."

The boy's form flickered, and another figure took his place—a woman, her features gaunt and her eyes hollow.

"Everything you could?" she asked, her voice sharp. "You abandoned us. You failed."

Kaelion staggered back, the weight of her words cutting through him like a blade. The figures multiplied, their voices rising into a cacophony of accusation and grief.

"You let us die."

"You weren't strong enough."

"You can't save anyone."

The voices grew louder, their weight pressing against Kaelion's chest until he could barely breathe. He fell to his knees, his hands gripping the ground as the reflections swirled around him.

"Enough!" he shouted, his voice raw.

The void fell silent.

Kaelion lifted his head, his breath coming in ragged gasps. The figures were gone, and the swirling sky above had stilled.

Selara stood before him, her violet eyes calm and steady.

"You can't carry it all," she said softly. "No one can."

Kaelion's gaze hardened. "I have to. If I don't, who will?"

Selara knelt before him, her expression gentle. "The world doesn't need a savior, Kaelion. It needs a weaver. Someone who can mend what's broken—not by force, but by trust."

Kaelion's chest tightened as her words sank in. He closed his eyes, the hum of the shard filling his senses.

"I don't know how," he whispered.

Selara placed a hand on his shoulder. "You do. You've always known."

The void shattered, and Kaelion was back in the chamber. He stood at the base of the shard, his hand resting against its surface. The resonance of the shard had changed—no longer chaotic, but steady, its energy weaving into a pattern that pulsed with quiet strength.

Tavriel approached cautiously, his staff glowing faintly. "You've aligned it," he said, his voice tinged with awe. "The shard's threads are steady once more."

Kaelion nodded, his chest heaving. "It's not just about strength. It's about trust. Balance isn't something we can force—it's something we have to weave together."

The group regrouped at the base of the shard, their expressions a mix of relief and exhaustion. The trial had tested them all, but the shard's resonance was now calm—a fragile thread in the fractured loom of the Axis.

Darith sheathed his blade, his brow furrowed. "That's one shard stabilized. But how many more are out there?"

Tavriel's gaze turned toward the horizon, his blind eyes thoughtful. "Each shard holds a piece of the loom. To mend the Axis, we must weave them all—but each thread carries its own trial."

Kaelion turned to the group, his voice steady. "Then we keep moving. The Axis won't wait for us."

The shard pulsed once more, its energy a faint but steady rhythm that echoed through the chamber. The loom of the world was far from whole—but for the first time, Kaelion felt a glimmer of hope.

And as they stepped out of the Woven Spire, the horizon stretched before them—a tapestry of light and shadow waiting to be rewoven.

# Chapter Eleven: The Shard's Shadow

The air outside the Woven Spire was cooler, the oppressive hum of the shard now replaced by a subtle, rhythmic pulse that seemed to follow them as they descended the foothills. The group moved in silence, the weight of their trial still heavy on their shoulders. The horizon stretched wide before them, its twilight hues shimmering with the faint glow of distant shards.

Kaelion walked at the front of the column, his gaze fixed on the landscape ahead. His thoughts churned with the echoes of the trial within the Spire, Selara's words lingering in his mind.

The world doesn't need a savior. It needs a weaver.

"Kaelion," Darith's voice cut through his reverie. The ranger's expression was grim as he pointed to a cluster of low, jagged hills in the distance. "We've got company."

Kaelion followed his gaze, his hand instinctively moving to the hilt of his sword. Figures moved among the hills, their forms faint but unmistakable.

"They're shard-forged," Tavriel said quietly, his blind eyes turned toward the distant threat. "The remnants of Cyrix's forces. They must have followed the resonance of the Spire."

Kaelion's jaw tightened. "How many?"

"Enough to make this messy," Darith replied, his tone dry. "And they're between us and the next shard."

The group halted at the edge of the foothills, their weapons drawn as they prepared for the inevitable confrontation. The shard-forged warriors moved closer, their forms twisted and unnatural, their weapons glowing with the chaotic energy of the Axis.

Kaelion stepped forward, his voice steady. "We hold the line here. No one gets through."

Darith grinned, his blade already drawn. "Now you're speaking my language."

Tavriel moved to the rear of the group, his staff glowing faintly as he began to chant. The air around him shimmered, a protective barrier of shadowlight forming to shield their flank.

"Focus on the cores," Kaelion said, his gaze sweeping over the group. "It's the only way to stop them."

The first wave of shard-forged warriors descended upon them moments later, their movements swift and precise.

Kaelion met the charge head-on, his blade cutting through the first warrior with a burst of light. The shard-forged creature dissolved into fragments, its chaotic energy dissipating into the air.

Darith fought beside him, his strikes quick and calculated. The ranger moved like a shadow, his blade finding the weaknesses in their enemies' defenses with practiced precision.

The battle was brutal and unrelenting, the shard-forged warriors fighting with an eerie, mechanical precision. Each one that fell was replaced by another, their numbers seemingly endless.

"Tavriel!" Kaelion shouted, parrying a blow from one of the warriors. "How much longer?"

The seer's voice was calm despite the chaos. "The barrier will hold—but not forever. The shard-forged aren't just fighting us. They're feeding on the energy of the Spire."

Kaelion's jaw tightened. He drove his blade through another warrior, the force of the strike sending a shockwave through the battlefield.

"Then we need to end this. Now."

The tide of the battle began to shift as the group fought with renewed determination. Kaelion moved with purpose, his strikes guided by the faint hum of the shard's resonance still lingering within him.

Darith's laughter echoed through the chaos as he dispatched another warrior. "You know, for twisted shard abominations, they're not bad sparring partners."

Kaelion gave him a wry look. "You can joke after we survive this."

"Survival's the best punchline," Darith quipped, grinning as he parried another attack.

The final wave of shard-forged warriors fell moments later, their forms dissolving into fragments of light and shadow that scattered across the battlefield.

Kaelion lowered his sword, his chest heaving as he scanned the area. The ground was littered with the remnants of their enemies, the air still crackling faintly with residual energy.

Darith sheathed his blade, his grin fading into a more serious expression. "That's twice now we've run into them. They're not just wandering—they're hunting."

Kaelion nodded, his gaze turning toward the distant horizon. "Cyrix may be gone, but his influence isn't. The shard-forged aren't just remnants. They're echoes of his intent—and they won't stop until the Axis is whole again."

The group regrouped at the base of a low ridge, their movements slow and deliberate as they tended to their injuries and checked their supplies. Tavriel stood at the edge of the camp, his staff planted firmly in the ground as he gazed toward the distant spires of light that marked the location of the next shard.

Kaelion approached him, his voice quiet. "What's waiting for us there?"

Tavriel didn't turn, his blind eyes fixed on the horizon. "The threads are fraying, Kaelion. Each shard we stabilize pulls the loom closer to balance—but the closer we get, the harder it will be to hold it together."

Kaelion's jaw tightened. "We don't have a choice."

Tavriel turned to him, his expression unreadable. "No. We don't. But choices will still be made. And not all threads can be saved."

The shard's pulse continued to echo faintly in the distance, its resonance a constant reminder of the trials yet to come. Kaelion stood at the edge of the camp, his gaze fixed on the shimmering spires of the next shard.

The weight of the Axis pressed against him, heavy and unrelenting. But as the first stars of the Eclipse began to pierce the twilight sky, he felt a flicker of resolve burn within him.

The loom was waiting.

And Kaelion would see it mended.

# Chapter Twelve: The Shard of Horizons

The journey to the next shard began before the first light of false dawn. The air was cool, tinged with the faint metallic taste of residual shard energy lingering from their battle the day before. The survivors moved in silence, their footsteps crunching softly against the rocky terrain. Ahead, the spires of light that marked the shard's location glimmered faintly on the horizon, a beacon of both hope and danger.

Kaelion walked at the front of the group, his expression resolute. Every step forward felt heavier, the weight of the Axis's broken threads pressing against him like an invisible hand. The echoes of their trials lingered in his mind—Selara's voice, the hum of the shard, the whispers of the loom.

"You're quiet," Darith said, falling into step beside him. The ranger's tone was light, but his eyes betrayed his concern. "That usually means you're thinking about something reckless."

Kaelion allowed himself a faint smile. "Just trying to figure out how we're going to survive this."

Darith snorted. "Survival's easy. It's the fixing-the-world part that's tricky."

Kaelion glanced at him, his smile fading. "One step at a time, Darith. That's all we can do."

The terrain grew harsher as they approached the shard's location, the ground beneath their feet giving way to jagged ridges and deep crevices that seemed to pulse faintly with chaotic energy. The spires of light loomed closer now, their glow illuminating the surrounding landscape in eerie, shifting patterns.

Tavriel paused at the edge of a wide fissure, his staff planted firmly in the ground as he turned his blind eyes toward the shard. "This shard is different," he said softly. "Its resonance is... fragmented. Unstable."

Kaelion frowned, stepping to his side. "What does that mean?"

Tavriel tilted his head, his expression thoughtful. "It means the loom is fraying faster here. The threads are tangled, twisted. The shard won't just test us—it will fight us."

"Great," Darith muttered from behind them. "Because we haven't had enough of that already."

Kaelion's jaw tightened as he turned to the group. "We've faced worse. We can handle this."

The group descended into the fissure, their movements cautious as they navigated the uneven terrain. The air grew heavier the closer they got to the shard, the hum of its resonance vibrating through the ground and filling their lungs with its electric tang.

The spires of light loomed above them now, their glow brighter and more erratic. Threads of light and shadow weaved through the air, their movements chaotic and unpredictable.

At the center of the fissure stood the shard—a towering fragment of shimmering energy that pulsed with every beat of the Axis. Its surface was jagged and uneven, the patterns etched into it twisting and writhing like living things.

Kaelion approached cautiously, his hand resting on the hilt of his sword. The shard's resonance pressed against him, its pull stronger than anything he had felt before.

"Whatever we do," he said quietly, "we do it fast. This shard isn't waiting for us."

The first sign of resistance came as they crossed the threshold into the shard's immediate radius. Threads of light and shadow unraveled from its surface, coalescing into swirling forms that moved with an almost predatory grace.

"They're back," Darith said, his blade already drawn.

Kaelion raised his sword, his gaze fixed on the forms. "Hold the line. Keep them away from the shard."

The forms attacked with a speed and ferocity that took them by surprise. Kaelion met the first one head-on, his blade cutting through its shifting threads with a burst of energy. The form dissolved into fragments, but more took its place, their movements coordinated and relentless.

Darith fought beside him, his strikes quick and precise. The ranger's blade cut through the forms with practiced efficiency, but even he was beginning to tire.

"There's too many of them!" Darith shouted, parrying another attack.

Kaelion gritted his teeth, his movements deliberate as he fought to hold the line. "We hold. No matter what."

Tavriel stood at the edge of the fray, his staff glowing faintly as he chanted a low, rhythmic incantation. The threads around him faltered, their movements slowing as the seer's magic disrupted their resonance.

"The shard's energy is amplifying them," Tavriel called out, his voice steady despite the strain. "We need to disrupt its flow  or they'll overwhelm us!"

Kaelion's gaze darted toward the shard, its surface glowing brighter with each passing moment. The patterns etched into it twisted and writhed, their movements growing more erratic as the battle raged on.

"Tavriel, can you stabilize it?" Kaelion shouted.

The seer hesitated, his expression grim. "Not from here. Someone has to get close enough to touch it—to guide its threads."

Kaelion's jaw tightened. "Then I'll do it."

The battlefield was a blur of chaos as Kaelion fought his way toward the shard. The forms converged on him, their movements growing faster and more coordinated as he drew closer. Each step felt heavier, the shard's pull growing stronger with every moment.

Darith's voice cut through the chaos. "Kaelion! You're not seriously—"

"I am," Kaelion interrupted, his tone firm. "Hold them off as long as you can."

The ranger cursed under his breath but nodded, turning his blade toward the oncoming swarm.

Kaelion reached the base of the shard, the hum of its resonance filling his mind like a deafening roar. He raised his hand, his fingers brushing against its surface.

The world shifted in an instant.

Kaelion found himself standing in an endless expanse of light and shadow, the ground beneath him rippling like water. The shard loomed before him, its surface glowing faintly as patterns of energy began to weave and unravel in chaotic loops.

A voice echoed through the void, sharp and resonant. "You seek to mend what is broken. But what will you sacrifice to make it whole?"

Kaelion's chest tightened as the patterns coalesced into a familiar form—Selara.

"You carry too much," she said, her voice soft but firm. "Let go, Kaelion. Or the loom will break beneath your weight."

He clenched his fists, his jaw tightening. "I can't let go. If I do, everything falls apart."

Selara stepped closer, her gaze steady. "Then show me. Prove that you can hold the threads together."

The patterns around him surged, their movements growing more erratic as the shard's resonance reached a fever pitch. Kaelion raised his sword, the hum of the Severance Stone's lingering energy vibrating through his bones.

He stepped forward, his voice steady. "I will."

The shard's light flared, and the void exploded into chaos.

# Chapter Thirteen: The Shard's Core

Kaelion stood alone within the void, the shard towering before him like a jagged star. The patterns of light and shadow etched into its surface twisted violently, each thread pulling against the others in a chaotic dance. The resonance of the shard was deafening now, filling the space around him with a low, thrumming vibration that threatened to tear him apart.

"You think you can weave this broken loom?" a voice echoed through the void, sharp and accusing. "You are as fractured as the Axis itself."

Kaelion's chest tightened as the voice took form. Before him stood a shadowy figure, its edges blurred and indistinct. Its face was his own, twisted into an expression of disdain.

"You couldn't save Solaris," the shadow said, stepping closer. "You couldn't save Selara. What makes you think you can save this world?"

Kaelion gripped his sword tightly, his jaw clenching. "I didn't come here to argue with myself."

The shadow laughed, its voice a mocking echo. "But that's exactly what you're doing. You can't weave the loom, Kaelion—not while you're unraveling yourself."

The shard pulsed violently, the threads of light and shadow flaring around Kaelion in chaotic bursts. The ground beneath him shifted, rippling like water as the resonance of the shard grew stronger.

Kaelion took a step forward, his gaze fixed on the towering fragment. The hum of the shard pressed against him, its energy seeping into his mind like an invasive whisper.

"You carry too much," the shadow said, circling him like a predator. "Your guilt. Your failures. Your need to fix what's broken. It will crush you, Kaelion. It already has."

Kaelion closed his eyes, the hum of the shard filling his senses. Memories surged to the surface—Selara's laughter, the screams of the innocent, the blinding light of Solaris's spires. Each one a thread, woven into the fabric of his purpose.

"You're right," Kaelion said quietly, his voice steady.

The shadow paused, its form flickering. "What?"

Kaelion opened his eyes, his gaze unwavering. "I am fractured. I've failed more times than I can count. But I'm still here."

The shadow's form wavered, its edges blurring. "And what does that mean?"

"It means I can still fight," Kaelion said, stepping forward. "It means I can still weave."

The shard flared, its light and shadow twisting into a violent storm that surged toward Kaelion. He raised his sword, the hum of the Severance Stone's lingering energy resonating through the blade.

The storm crashed against him, its force driving him to his knees. The weight of the shard's energy pressed against his chest, each thread pulling in a different direction.

"You can't hold it all," the shadow said, its voice sharp and mocking.

"I don't have to," Kaelion said through gritted teeth.

He reached out, his hand brushing against the shard's surface. The chaotic energy surged through him, filling his mind with a blinding light.

Kaelion found himself standing in a new void, this one calm and still. The shard floated before him, its surface glowing faintly as its threads began to stabilize.

Selara appeared beside him, her expression calm and steady.

"You've learned," she said softly. "The loom isn't about holding everything together. It's about letting the threads find their place."

Kaelion nodded, his chest heaving. "It's about trust."

Selara smiled, her form beginning to fade. "Then trust yourself."

The void shattered, and Kaelion was back in the fissure. The shard's resonance had changed—no longer chaotic, but steady. Its surface glowed with a soft, unified light, the threads etched into it weaving together in intricate patterns.

Kaelion stepped back, his chest heaving as he lowered his hand. The hum of the shard was quieter now, its energy no longer oppressive but comforting.

Tavriel approached cautiously, his staff glowing faintly. "You've stabilized it," he said, his voice tinged with awe. "The threads are woven."

Kaelion nodded, his gaze fixed on the shard. "It's not just the shard. It's me. The loom doesn't need a savior—it needs a weaver."

The group regrouped at the base of the shard, their expressions a mix of relief and exhaustion. Darith leaned against a jagged rock, his blade sheathed but his stance still tense.

"Two shards down," he said, his tone dry. "How many more to go?"

Tavriel tilted his head, his expression thoughtful. "Enough to test every thread of our resolve. The loom is far from whole."

Kaelion turned to the group, his voice steady. "Then we keep moving. The Axis won't wait for us."

The shard's light pulsed faintly, its resonance a steady rhythm that echoed through the fissure. The horizon stretched wide before them, the distant spires of the next shard glimmering faintly in the twilight.

Kaelion stood at the edge of the group, his gaze fixed on the path ahead. The weight of the Axis pressed against him, but for the first time, he felt something else—a quiet, fragile hope.

The loom was waiting.

And Kaelion would see it mended.

# Chapter Fourteen: Fragments of the Past

The twilight deepened as the group moved on, leaving the glowing shard behind in its steady hum. The air was cooler now, the oppressive weight of the shard's chaotic energy replaced by a quiet, fragile stillness. Each step forward felt like a reprieve, but also a reminder of the trials yet to come.

Kaelion walked at the front, his gaze fixed on the distant horizon where the faint glow of the next shard shimmered. The threads of light and shadow it emitted wove across the sky like fleeting constellations, a silent promise of both challenge and hope.

Behind him, Darith let out a low whistle, breaking the heavy silence. "You know, I used to think hunting wild beasts in the Twilight Marches was tough. But this? This is something else entirely."

Kaelion allowed himself a faint smile. "Would you rather go back?"

Darith chuckled. "Not a chance. I just miss the days when I didn't have to think about saving the world every five minutes."

They made camp at the edge of a narrow valley, its rocky terrain offering some protection from the open sky. A faint wind swept through the area, carrying the scent of earth and distant rain.

Kaelion sat by the fire, his sword resting across his knees as he stared into the flames. The faint hum of the stabilized shard still lingered in his senses, a reminder of what they had achieved—and what they still had to face.

Tavriel sat nearby, his staff planted in the ground beside him. The seer's blind eyes seemed to glow faintly in the firelight, his expression contemplative.

"You're carrying it differently now," Tavriel said, his voice soft.

Kaelion glanced at him, his brow furrowed. "What do you mean?"

"The weight," Tavriel said. "It's still there, but it's not breaking you. You've found a thread to hold onto—a purpose."

Kaelion's gaze returned to the fire. "It's not about me. It never was. The Axis doesn't care about what I've lost, or what I'm afraid of. It's about the loom. About making it whole again."

Tavriel nodded, a faint smile touching his lips. "You're starting to understand."

As the group settled into a quiet rhythm, Darith approached the fire, dropping a bundle of kindling onto the flames. He leaned against a nearby rock, his expression unusually serious.

"Do you ever think about what comes next?" Darith asked, his voice low.

Kaelion frowned. "What do you mean?"

Darith gestured vaguely toward the horizon. "After this. After the shards, the Axis, all of it. What happens then? Do we just go back to... whatever was left of our lives before?"

Kaelion was silent for a moment, his thoughts turning to Solaris, to Selara, to the fractured remnants of the world they were fighting to save.

"I don't know," he admitted. "But if we don't see this through, there won't be anything to go back to."

Darith nodded, his expression thoughtful. "Fair point. Just don't forget—saving the world doesn't mean much if there's no one left to live in it."

The conversation was interrupted by a sudden shift in the air. A faint hum filled the valley, distant but unmistakable. Kaelion rose to his feet, his hand going to the hilt of his sword.

"It's the shard," Tavriel said, his voice calm but firm. "The next one is waking."

The group moved quickly, gathering their supplies and preparing for the journey ahead. The glow on the horizon grew brighter as they approached, the hum of the shard's resonance growing louder with each step.

The valley opened into a wide plain, its surface dotted with jagged rock formations that pulsed faintly with shard energy. The shard itself stood at the center of the plain, its form taller and more fractured than the last. Threads of light and shadow spiraled around it, their movements chaotic and unsteady.

"This one feels... different," Darith said, his voice tinged with unease.

"It is," Tavriel replied. "The resonance is frayed. The threads are tangled—and they're pulling against each other."

Kaelion stepped forward, his gaze fixed on the shard. The hum of its energy pressed against him, filling his chest with a sense of urgency.

"Then we untangle them," he said.

As they approached the shard, the air around it began to ripple. The threads of light and shadow spiraling around its surface unraveled, forming into shifting, humanoid shapes that moved with an eerie grace.

"More shard-forged," Darith muttered, drawing his blade. "Of course."

Kaelion raised his sword, his voice steady. "Hold the line. Keep them away from the shard."

The shard-forged attacked with relentless precision, their movements swift and unpredictable. Kaelion met them head-on, his blade cutting through their shifting forms with bursts of light.

Darith fought at his side, his strikes quick and decisive. The ranger moved like a shadow, his blade finding the vulnerabilities in their enemies' defenses with practiced ease.

Tavriel remained at the edge of the fray, his staff glowing faintly as he worked to disrupt the shard-forged's resonance. The air around him shimmered, a protective barrier of shadowlight forming to shield the group.

"The shard's energy is feeding them," Tavriel called out. "If we don't stabilize it, they'll overwhelm us!"

Kaelion's gaze darted toward the shard, its surface glowing brighter with each passing moment. The patterns etched into it twisted violently, their movements growing more erratic.

"Tavriel, can you guide the threads?" Kaelion shouted.

The seer hesitated, his expression grim. "Not alone. Someone needs to align them."

Kaelion nodded, his jaw tightening. "Then I'll do it."

The battlefield was chaos as Kaelion fought his way toward the shard. The shard-forged converged on him, their attacks growing more coordinated and ferocious. Each step forward felt heavier, the shard's resonance pressing against him like an invisible weight.

He reached the base of the shard, its energy crackling around him like a storm. He raised his hand, his fingers brushing against its surface.

The world shifted.

Kaelion found himself in a void of shifting light and shadow, the shard's core glowing faintly before him. The threads spiraling around it were tangled and frayed, their movements chaotic and erratic.

A voice echoed through the void, sharp and resonant. "You seek to mend what is broken. But what will you sacrifice to make it whole?"

Kaelion's chest tightened as the threads began to weave into familiar shapes. Selara. Solaris. The faces of the fallen.

The voice grew louder. "What will you sacrifice?"

Kaelion clenched his fists, his voice steady. "Whatever it takes."

The threads surged toward him, their chaotic energy pressing against him like a wave. He stepped forward, his hand reaching for the shard's core.

"I will weave," he said, his voice firm.

The shard's light flared, and the void exploded into blinding brilliance.

# Chapter Fifteen: The Fractured Loom

Kaelion opened his eyes to the void, the brilliance of the shard's light fading into a muted glow. Threads of energy spiraled around him, their movements slowing as the chaotic hum of the shard began to steady. The vast expanse of the void pulsed faintly, each beat resonating in his chest.

At the heart of the space stood the shard's core—a jagged fragment of shimmering energy that glowed with an unearthly light. The threads surrounding it moved with purpose now, weaving into intricate patterns that flickered with the faint promise of unity.

"You've reached the loom's edge," a voice said softly.

Kaelion turned to see Tavriel standing beside him, his blind eyes glowing faintly. The seer's presence was steady, a quiet beacon in the storm of energy.

"What happens now?" Kaelion asked, his voice low.

Tavriel tilted his head, his expression thoughtful. "The shard is stabilizing, but it's not whole. Its threads are still fractured, and they will demand something more from you. A choice."

Kaelion frowned, his grip on his sword tightening. "What kind of choice?"

"The kind that tests what you're willing to sacrifice," Tavriel said.

The void shifted, and the shard's energy surged, the threads spiraling outward in chaotic loops. The space around Kaelion began to warp, and for a moment, he felt as though the ground beneath him was falling away.

The threads coalesced into shapes, their forms familiar and haunting. Selara's face appeared first, her violet eyes gleaming with a mixture of sorrow and resolve. Behind her stood the blurred figures of the innocents Kaelion had failed to save, their silent gazes heavy with accusation.

"You carry us," Selara said, her voice calm but piercing. "Every thread you've broken, every choice you've made—they weigh on you."

Kaelion's chest tightened. "I don't have a choice. If I let go, everything falls apart."

"You can't weave with broken threads," Selara said softly. "You have to mend them—or sever them."

The shard pulsed again, its light flaring as the figures dissolved into swirling threads. The patterns shifted, their movements becoming sharper, more erratic.

Kaelion felt a pull deep within his chest, the shard's resonance pressing against him like an invisible hand. The threads around him began to tighten, their energy coiling into a lattice that shimmered with both light and shadow.

"This is the test," Tavriel said, his voice steady. "The shard is calling for balance. It's not just about weaving—it's about choosing which threads to keep, and which to let go."

Kaelion closed his eyes, the hum of the shard filling his mind. Memories surged to the surface—of Selara, of Solaris, of every moment that had brought him to this point. Each memory was a thread, woven into the fabric of his purpose.

"What will you sacrifice?" the voice echoed again, resonating through the void.

Kaelion opened his eyes, his jaw tightening. "I'll sacrifice what I must—but not what I am."

The void trembled, and the threads surged toward the shard's core. Kaelion stepped forward, his sword glowing faintly with the lingering energy of the Severance Stone. He raised the blade, its resonance aligning with the shard's chaotic hum.

The threads lashed out, their energy cutting through the air like living things. Kaelion moved with purpose, his strikes precise and deliberate. Each thread he severed dissolved into light, its chaotic energy dissipating into the void.

The shard's resonance grew louder, its patterns becoming more stable with each moment. Kaelion's movements slowed as the final threads wove together, their intricate lattice forming a unified whole.

The shard pulsed once more, its light softening into a steady glow. The void stilled, the chaotic hum fading into silence.

Kaelion found himself back in the plain, the shard standing before him. Its surface was no longer jagged and chaotic, but smooth and steady, its light glowing with a quiet strength.

Tavriel stood nearby, his staff glowing faintly. The seer's expression was calm, his blind eyes focused on the shard.

"You've mended this thread," Tavriel said softly. "But the loom is far from whole."

Kaelion nodded, his chest heaving as he sheathed his sword. "Then we keep moving. There are more shards to stabilize."

Darith approached from the edge of the battlefield, his blade resting on his shoulder. His expression was weary but resolute.

"Every time I think we're getting closer, the Axis throws another twist at us," Darith said, his tone dry. "You sure we're not just chasing ghosts?"

Kaelion allowed himself a faint smile. "If we are, they're ghosts worth chasing."

The group regrouped at the edge of the plain, their movements slow but purposeful. The shard's steady hum filled the air, a quiet reminder of the progress they had made.

Kaelion stood at the edge of the group, his gaze fixed on the distant horizon. The faint glow of the next shard shimmered in the twilight, its threads weaving a pattern that seemed to call to him.

The loom was waiting.

And Kaelion would see it mended.

# Chapter Sixteen: The Loom Unravels

The trek toward the next shard was grueling. The landscape shifted from jagged ridges to an expanse of ash-covered plains, the ground brittle and cracked beneath their feet. The air was thick with the scent of scorched earth, a reminder of the battles that had scarred this land in ages past.

Kaelion led the group in silence, his focus sharp as his eyes scanned the horizon. The faint glow of the shard pulsed in the distance, its light flickering like a faltering star. Tavriel followed close behind, his staff clicking softly against the ground with every step.

"This place is wrong," Darith muttered, his gaze sweeping the desolate terrain. "The air feels... heavy."

"It's the shard," Tavriel replied. "Its resonance is out of sync with the Axis. The threads here are pulling against each other, unraveling the weave."

Kaelion's jaw tightened. "Then we need to reach it before it falls apart completely."

The group descended into a shallow valley, its walls carved with strange, angular markings that glowed faintly in the twilight. The ground beneath them hummed with a faint vibration, the shard's chaotic energy seeping into every crevice.

At the heart of the valley, the shard stood atop a jagged outcrop of stone. Its surface was fractured and unstable, threads of light and shadow spiraling around it in violent, erratic patterns. The hum of its resonance was louder here, a low, discordant thrum that pressed against their senses like an unrelenting tide.

Kaelion stepped forward, his hand resting on the hilt of his sword. "We stabilize it, just like the others."

Tavriel's expression was grave. "This shard is different. Its resonance isn't just chaotic—it's consuming the threads around it. If we don't act quickly, the entire weave could collapse."

As they approached the shard, the ground beneath their feet began to shift. Threads of light and shadow unraveled from the shard's surface, coalescing into twisted, jagged forms that moved with an unnatural grace.

"They're back," Darith said, drawing his blade. "And they're uglier than ever."

Kaelion raised his sword, his voice steady. "Hold the line. Keep them away from the shard."

The forms attacked with ferocity, their movements erratic and unpredictable. Kaelion met the first wave head-on, his blade cutting through their shifting threads with bursts of light. Each strike sent ripples through the air, the shard's resonance vibrating in response.

Darith fought at his side, his strikes quick and precise. The ranger moved like a shadow, his blade finding the weaknesses in their enemies' defenses with practiced ease.

"This is worse than before," Darith called out, parrying another attack. "They're not just fighting us—they're feeding off the shard's energy."

Kaelion gritted his teeth, his movements deliberate as he pushed forward. "Then we shut them down. Tavriel, can you weaken them?"

The seer stood at the edge of the fray, his staff glowing faintly as he chanted a low, rhythmic incantation. The air around him shimmered, a web of shadowlight spreading outward to disrupt the shard-forged's resonance.

"They're tied to the shard," Tavriel said, his voice strained. "If we stabilize it, they'll fall."

The battle was relentless, the shard-forged attacking in unending waves. Kaelion's strikes grew heavier with each moment, the weight of the shard's chaotic energy pressing against him like an invisible force.

The shard flared suddenly, its light and shadow twisting into a violent storm that surged outward. The ground beneath them trembled, cracks spreading through the brittle earth.

"Kaelion!" Tavriel shouted, his voice cutting through the chaos. "The shard is destabilizing. If we don't act now—"

Kaelion didn't let him finish. He fought his way toward the shard, his movements deliberate as he cut through the shard-forged that stood in his path. Each step forward felt like a battle in itself, the shard's resonance pulling at him with every moment.

He reached the base of the shard, the storm of energy surrounding it crackling against his skin. The threads spiraling around its surface were tangled and frayed, their movements erratic and unstable.

Kaelion raised his hand, his fingers brushing against the shard's surface.

The world shifted.

Kaelion found himself standing in an expanse of darkness, the shard's core glowing faintly before him. The threads surrounding it were tangled and broken, their patterns shifting and collapsing in on themselves.

A voice echoed through the void, sharp and resonant. "You seek to mend what is broken. But what will you surrender to make it whole?"

Kaelion's chest tightened as the threads began to weave into shapes. Faces appeared before him—Selara, Darith, Tavriel, the fallen soldiers of Solaris. Their gazes were heavy with expectation, their voices silent but deafening.

"What will you surrender?" the voice repeated.

Kaelion closed his eyes, the hum of the shard filling his mind. Memories surged to the surface—of his failures, his triumphs, the weight of every decision he had made.

When he opened his eyes, his jaw was set. "I'll surrender what's needed—but I won't lose who I am."

The threads surged toward him, their chaotic energy pressing against him like a wave. Kaelion raised his sword, its resonance aligning with the shard's hum.

"I will weave," he said, his voice steady.

The threads coiled around him, their energy seeping into his mind and body. Kaelion moved with purpose, his strikes deliberate as he cut through the chaos, severing the broken threads and weaving the stable ones into place.

The shard's resonance grew quieter, its patterns stabilizing with each movement. The chaotic energy surrounding it began to fade, the void stilling as the threads wove together into a unified whole.

Kaelion opened his eyes to the valley, the shard standing before him. Its surface was smooth and steady now, its light glowing with a quiet strength.

Tavriel approached cautiously, his staff glowing faintly. "You've aligned the threads," he said, his voice tinged with awe. "The shard is whole again."

Kaelion nodded, his chest heaving as he sheathed his sword. "But the loom isn't."

Darith stepped forward, his expression weary but resolute. "So what's next? Another shard? Another test?"

Kaelion's gaze turned toward the horizon, where the faint glow of the next shard shimmered in the twilight. "The loom is waiting," he said quietly.

"And we're not done yet."

# Chapter Seventeen: The Shard of Echoes

The horizon was bathed in twilight as the group made their way toward the next shard. The ground beneath their feet shifted from brittle rock to soft, silty soil that whispered with every step. In the distance, faint echoes reverberated across the plain—unseen whispers carried by a wind that did not stir the air.

Kaelion paused at the crest of a low ridge, his gaze fixed on the faint glow of the shard ahead. Its light was softer than the others, its resonance carrying a melodic hum that tugged at the edges of his thoughts.

"This place feels... different," Darith muttered, his voice low. "Quieter. But not in a good way."

Tavriel stood beside him, his blind eyes glowing faintly as he tilted his head toward the shard. "It's not quiet," the seer said softly. "It's listening."

Kaelion frowned, his hand resting on the hilt of his sword. "Listening for what?"

Tavriel turned his gaze toward the shard, his expression unreadable. "For us."

The shard stood at the heart of a shallow basin, its surface smooth and reflective. Threads of light and shadow spiraled lazily around it, their movements calm and deliberate. The hum of its resonance filled the air, a low, melodic vibration that seemed to resonate within the very fabric of the world.

Kaelion approached cautiously, his footsteps muffled by the soft soil. The shard's presence was overwhelming, its energy pressing against him with a strange, almost inviting warmth.

As he reached the edge of the basin, the air around him grew heavy. The echoes that had lingered in the distance grew louder, their voices overlapping in a chaotic symphony.

"Do you hear that?" Darith asked, his voice tight.

Kaelion nodded, his jaw tightening. "Voices. Hundreds of them."

"It's the shard," Tavriel said, his tone calm but firm. "It holds the echoes of those who have touched it—every thread it's ever woven. They're reaching out to us."

The voices grew louder as they approached the shard, their tones layered and indistinct. Words formed and dissolved in an instant, leaving behind fragments of meaning that lingered in the air like the remnants of a dream.

Kaelion stopped a few paces from the shard, his gaze fixed on its reflective surface. For a moment, he thought he saw his own face staring back at him—but the reflection shifted, its features softening into the visage of Selara.

Her lips moved, but the words were lost in the cacophony of echoes.

Kaelion clenched his fists, his voice sharp. "What do you want from us?"

The shard's light flared, and the voices fell silent.

The silence was brief.

The ground beneath their feet trembled, and the threads of light and shadow surrounding the shard unraveled. The air grew colder, and the melodic hum of the shard shifted into a low, discordant vibration that pressed against their senses.

Darith drew his blade, his stance tense. "Here we go again."

The threads coalesced into shifting forms, their movements fluid and unnatural. They circled the group with predatory grace, their features indistinct and ever-changing.

"These aren't shard-forged," Tavriel said, his voice edged with unease. "They're echoes—reflections of the loom itself."

Kaelion raised his sword, his voice steady. "Reflections or not, they're not stopping us."

The battle was unlike anything they had faced before. The echoes moved with an eerie precision, their attacks swift and unpredictable. Kaelion's sword cut through the first form, but instead of dissipating, it fractured into smaller, faster fragments that surged toward him with renewed ferocity.

Darith fought beside him, his strikes precise and calculated. The ranger gritted his teeth as he parried another attack. "These things don't go down easy!"

"They're not meant to," Tavriel said from the edge of the fray, his staff glowing faintly as he chanted a low incantation. "They're testing us—forcing us to confront the threads we've left behind."

Kaelion's movements slowed as the echoes shifted, their forms taking on familiar shapes. Faces from his past appeared before him—soldiers from Solaris, villagers from the Broken Step, Selara's violet eyes glimmering with quiet judgment.

"You can't save us," the echoes whispered, their voices overlapping in a haunting refrain.

Kaelion staggered back, his breath catching in his chest. The shard's resonance grew louder, its discordant hum vibrating through his bones.

Tavriel's voice cut through the chaos. "Kaelion! You have to align the threads. The shard won't stabilize until you confront what it's showing you."

Kaelion gritted his teeth, his gaze fixed on the shard. The faces of the echoes swirled around him, their voices rising into a deafening crescendo.

"I can't save everyone," he said quietly, his voice steady despite the storm of emotion.

The echoes faltered, their movements slowing.

"I failed," Kaelion continued, his chest tightening. "But I'm still here. And I can still fight."

The shard's resonance shifted, its discordant hum softening into a steady rhythm. The echoes dissolved into threads of light and shadow, their energy spiraling back toward the shard's core.

Kaelion stepped forward, his hand brushing against the shard's surface. The world around him shifted, and he found himself standing in a void of endless light and shadow. The shard floated before him, its threads weaving into intricate patterns that flickered with the promise of unity.

"You seek to mend the loom," a voice echoed, calm and resonant. "But what will you sacrifice to make it whole?"

Kaelion's chest tightened as the patterns shifted, forming into familiar shapes. Selara. Darith. Tavriel. The faces of those who had fought and fallen.

"I'll sacrifice what I must," he said quietly. "But I won't lose the threads that matter."

The shard's light flared, and the void dissolved into blinding brilliance.

Kaelion opened his eyes to the basin, the shard standing before him. Its surface was smooth and reflective now, its light glowing with a quiet strength.

Tavriel approached cautiously, his staff glowing faintly. "You've stabilized it," he said softly. "The echoes are quiet."

Kaelion nodded, his chest heaving as he lowered his hand. "The loom isn't just threads. It's voices. Lives. And we can't mend it by forgetting them."

Darith approached, his expression weary but resolute. "Three shards down. How many more to go?"

Kaelion's gaze turned toward the horizon, where the faint glow of the next shard shimmered in the twilight.

"As many as it takes," he said.

# Chapter Eighteen: The Woven Tempest

The wind carried a strange, sharp chill as the group approached the next shard. The landscape shifted into a barren wasteland of cracked, glassy earth that glinted like molten obsidian under the twilight sky. In the distance, a storm brewed—thick, churning clouds of silver and black, their edges illuminated by crackling arcs of energy. At the storm's center stood the shard, its light flickering wildly as it pulsed with chaotic intensity.

Kaelion tightened his grip on his sword, his gaze locked on the storm. The resonance of the shard was palpable even from this distance, its vibrations rippling through the air like an invisible tide.

"This is worse than the others," Tavriel said softly, his blind eyes focused on the storm. "The threads here aren't just frayed—they're tearing apart."

Darith let out a low whistle, his tone laced with unease. "And we're just walking into that, are we?"

Kaelion glanced at him, his expression resolute. "We don't have a choice. If the threads tear, the Axis won't hold."

The storm's intensity grew as they neared the shard, the air thick with static that prickled against their skin. The ground trembled beneath their feet, and the hum of the shard's resonance grew louder, its chaotic energy pressing against them like a physical force.

Kaelion stopped at the edge of the storm, his gaze fixed on the swirling threads of light and shadow that spiraled around the shard.

They moved with violent, erratic precision, their patterns clashing and unraveling as they fought against each other.

"This isn't a trial," Tavriel said, his voice strained. "It's a battlefield. The threads are warring with each other, and we're caught in the middle."

Kaelion nodded, his jaw tightening. "Then we fight. Tavriel, can you guide the threads?"

The seer hesitated, his staff glowing faintly. "I can try—but their pull is strong. It will take everything we have to stabilize them."

The ground erupted as they stepped into the storm's radius, threads of light and shadow unraveling from the shard and coalescing into monstrous forms. These were no echoes or shard-forged—they were raw, chaotic energy made flesh, their movements erratic and violent.

Kaelion met the first form head-on, his sword slicing through its shifting threads with a burst of light. The creature dissolved into fragments, but its energy surged toward the shard, amplifying its resonance.

"They're feeding it!" Darith shouted, parrying an attack from another creature. "The more we fight, the stronger it gets!"

Kaelion cursed under his breath, his mind racing. "Tavriel! Can you contain it?"

Tavriel stood at the edge of the fray, his staff planted firmly in the ground as he chanted a low, rhythmic incantation. The air around him shimmered, a web of shadowlight spreading outward to disrupt the shard's chaotic resonance.

"It's fighting me," Tavriel said through gritted teeth. "The threads are too unstable—they're pulling in every direction at once."

Kaelion drove his blade through another creature, its form dissolving into threads that spiraled back toward the shard. The storm intensified, its winds howling as arcs of energy crackled through the air.

"We can't keep this up," Darith called out, his strikes growing slower as he fought to hold the line. "We need another plan!"

Kaelion's gaze darted toward the shard, its light flickering wildly as its resonance grew louder. The threads surrounding it were tangled and frayed, their movements chaotic and violent.

"We stabilize the shard," Kaelion said, his voice steady. "It's the only way."

Tavriel's voice was sharp. "You'll need to align the core threads—but the storm won't make it easy. It will test you."

Kaelion nodded, his grip on his sword tightening. "Then let it."

The storm surged as Kaelion fought his way toward the shard, the winds tearing at his armor and the chaotic energy pressing against him like an unrelenting tide. The creatures surrounding the shard converged on him, their attacks growing faster and more coordinated.

Kaelion's movements were deliberate, each strike a calculated effort to cut through the chaos. The shard loomed before him, its surface glowing with a violent, fractured light that pulsed in time with the storm.

He reached the base of the shard, the storm's energy crackling against his skin. The threads spiraling around its surface lashed out, their movements erratic and unpredictable.

Kaelion raised his hand, his fingers brushing against the shard's surface.

The world shifted.

Kaelion found himself in a void of swirling light and shadow, the shard's core glowing faintly before him. The threads surrounding it were tangled and torn, their movements violent and chaotic.

A voice echoed through the void, sharp and resonant. "The loom unravels. The weave collapses. What will you sacrifice to hold it together?"

Kaelion's chest tightened as the threads coiled around him, their energy pressing against him like a vice. Memories surged to the surface—of battles fought and lost, of choices made and regretted.

Each memory was a thread, frayed and fragile, woven into the fabric of his purpose.

"I'll sacrifice what's needed," he said quietly, his voice steady. "But I won't lose myself."

The threads surged toward him, their energy seeping into his mind and body. Kaelion moved with purpose, his strikes precise as he cut through the chaos, severing the broken threads and weaving the stable ones into place.

The shard's resonance shifted, its chaotic hum softening into a steady rhythm. The storm around him began to fade, the threads spiraling into intricate patterns that wove together into a unified whole.

Kaelion opened his eyes to the storm-torn battlefield, the shard standing before him. Its surface was smooth and steady now, its light glowing with a quiet strength.

The winds had stilled, and the ground beneath their feet was calm. The creatures born of the shard's chaos had dissolved, their energy fading into the air.

Tavriel approached cautiously, his staff glowing faintly. "You've woven the threads," he said softly. "The storm has passed."

Kaelion nodded, his chest heaving as he lowered his hand. "The loom isn't done. But this thread holds."

Darith stepped forward, his expression weary but resolute. "Four shards down. How many more?"

Kaelion's gaze turned toward the horizon, where the faint glow of the next shard shimmered in the distance.

"As many as it takes," he said quietly.

# Chapter Nineteen: Threads of Betrayal

The storm had long passed, but its lingering presence seemed etched into the landscape. The ground beneath the group's feet was scarred, blackened by the shard's chaotic energy. They moved cautiously now, the air thick with an unnatural stillness that set their nerves on edge.

Kaelion's gaze stayed fixed on the horizon, where the faint glow of the next shard shimmered like a distant star. Each shard they stabilized brought them closer to mending the Axis, but it also frayed the edges of their resolve.

Tavriel walked behind him, his staff clicking softly against the ground. The seer's face was drawn, his blind eyes faintly glowing. "Something is shifting," he said quietly. "The threads are... resisting us."

Darith frowned, his tone laced with suspicion. "Resisting? What does that mean?"

Tavriel's grip on his staff tightened. "The loom doesn't weave without cost. The closer we come to balance, the harder it will fight to hold its fractured state."

Kaelion slowed his pace, his jaw tightening. "Then we push through. No matter what."

The group entered a narrow canyon, its jagged walls towering high above them. The faint glow of the shard was brighter now, casting the canyon in a shifting light that seemed to ripple like water. The hum of the shard's resonance echoed faintly, its energy vibrating through the stone.

Kaelion led the way, his hand resting on the hilt of his sword. Each step forward felt heavier, the shard's pull growing stronger with every moment.

"This canyon is too quiet," Darith muttered, his gaze darting to the shadows. "It feels like a trap."

"It might be," Tavriel said, his tone calm but firm. "The shards test us in different ways. Be ready."

They reached a bend in the canyon, where the path opened into a wide chamber. At its center stood the shard, its surface smooth and reflective. Threads of light and shadow spiraled around it in slow, deliberate patterns, their movements hypnotic.

Kaelion stepped forward, his gaze fixed on the shard. The air around it felt thick, heavy with an unspoken tension.

"This feels wrong," Tavriel said softly, his voice edged with unease.

Kaelion glanced at him. "What is it?"

Tavriel hesitated, his blind eyes narrowing. "The shard's resonance is... incomplete. Something is interfering with it."

The tension snapped like a bowstring.

The ground beneath them trembled, and the threads surrounding the shard unraveled, their energy surging outward in chaotic bursts. Figures emerged from the shadows—human and inhuman alike, their forms twisted and warped by the shard's chaotic energy.

Darith drew his blade, his voice sharp. "Shard-forged?"

Tavriel shook his head, his staff glowing faintly. "No. These are... something else."

Kaelion raised his sword, his voice steady. "Hold the line. Protect the shard."

The figures attacked with brutal precision, their movements erratic and unpredictable. Kaelion met them head-on, his blade cutting through their forms with bursts of light. Each strike sent ripples through the air, the shard's resonance vibrating in response.

Darith fought at his side, his strikes quick and decisive. The ranger gritted his teeth as he parried another attack. "This isn't just chaos. Someone's controlling them."

Kaelion's focus shifted to the far side of the chamber, where a figure stepped forward from the shadows. The figure was clad in dark, shimmering armor that seemed to absorb the shard's light, its edges crackling with energy.

Kaelion's chest tightened as recognition struck. "Liora?"

The figure removed her helmet, revealing the face of Liora Delys. Her eyes glimmered with a strange, fractured light, her expression a mixture of anger and sorrow.

"You're too late, Kaelion," she said, her voice sharp. "The shard is already mine."

Kaelion lowered his sword slightly, his brow furrowing. "What are you doing, Liora? This isn't you."

She laughed, the sound bitter and hollow. "Isn't it? You think I wanted this? You think I chose to become part of this broken loom?"

Her gaze hardened, and the threads surrounding the shard coiled around her like living things. "I'm not trying to destroy the Axis, Kaelion. I'm trying to control it. To shape it into something better. Something stronger."

Kaelion's jaw tightened. "The Axis isn't meant to be controlled. You know that."

Liora's expression darkened. "And what do you think you're doing? You're just another thread trying to force the loom into place. But you don't see the bigger picture."

The battle erupted into chaos as Liora unleashed the shard's energy, the threads spiraling outward in violent, erratic bursts. The figures she commanded surged forward, their attacks growing more coordinated and precise.

Kaelion fought his way toward her, his movements deliberate as he cut through the chaos. Each step forward felt heavier, the shard's resonance pressing against him like an invisible weight.

"Liora!" he shouted, his voice cutting through the fray. "This isn't the way!"

She turned to face him, her expression cold. "You don't understand, Kaelion. You never did."

The shard flared, its light and shadow twisting into a violent storm that filled the chamber. The ground beneath them trembled, cracks spreading through the brittle stone.

Kaelion raised his sword, his voice steady. "Then make me understand."

The storm surged as Kaelion reached the base of the shard, its energy crackling against his skin. The threads surrounding it lashed out, their movements erratic and unpredictable.

Liora stood at the center of the chaos, her armor glowing with the shard's energy. Her gaze locked on Kaelion, and for a moment, her expression softened.

"You think you can save this world," she said, her voice quiet. "But it's already too far gone."

Kaelion stepped closer, his jaw tightening. "Then help me prove you wrong."

The shard's resonance shifted, its chaotic hum softening into a steady rhythm. The threads spiraling around it began to stabilize, their movements growing slower and more deliberate.

Liora hesitated, her grip on the shard faltering. "I... I don't know if I can."

Kaelion extended his hand, his voice steady. "You don't have to do this alone."

The shard's light flared, and the storm began to fade. The figures surrounding them dissolved into threads of light and shadow, their energy spiraling back toward the shard's core.

Liora lowered her gaze, her armor dimming as the shard's energy receded. She took a shaky step back, her voice barely a whisper. "I'm sorry."

Kaelion nodded, his chest heaving as he lowered his sword. "The loom is still waiting, Liora. We can mend it together."

The shard stood silent now, its surface smooth and reflective. Its resonance was steady, a quiet hum that filled the chamber with a sense of fragile peace.

Darith approached cautiously, his blade still in hand. "That was... unexpected."

Kaelion glanced at Liora, her expression heavy with guilt. "She's not our enemy. Not anymore."

Tavriel stepped forward, his staff glowing faintly. "The threads have shifted. But the weave is still incomplete."

Kaelion nodded, his gaze turning toward the horizon. The faint glow of the next shard shimmered in the distance, a silent reminder of the trials yet to come.

"And we're not done yet."

# Chapter Twenty: The Shard of Twilight

The sky above was painted in gradients of violet and deep gold, the perpetual twilight of the Marches stretching endlessly in every direction. The group moved cautiously through the stardust plains, their footsteps muffled by the soft, glowing grass that shimmered faintly beneath their weight.

Kaelion led the way, his gaze fixed on the horizon where the glow of the next shard pulsed faintly, its resonance weaving through the air like a distant song. Each step forward seemed to carry a deeper weight, the shard's energy pressing against them like an invisible tide.

Liora walked a few paces behind him, her expression distant. The glow of the shard still lingered faintly on her armor, a reminder of the power she had once tried to control.

"It feels strange," she said softly, her voice breaking the silence.

Kaelion glanced back at her, his brow furrowing. "What does?"

"The shards," Liora said, her gaze fixed on the horizon. "They don't just test us—they reflect us. Each one shows us something we're afraid to face."

Darith snorted, his tone dry. "Great. More existential nightmares. Just what we need."

The shard's glow grew brighter as they approached, its light weaving through the twilight in intricate patterns that danced across the plains. The air grew cooler, the faint scent of wild lavender carried on the wind.

Tavriel stopped suddenly, his staff planting firmly into the ground. His blind eyes glimmered faintly, his expression contemplative.

"We're close," he said softly. "This shard... it's different."

Kaelion turned to him, his hand resting on the hilt of his sword. "How?"

Tavriel tilted his head, his gaze distant. "Its threads aren't just woven into the loom. They're woven into us."

Liora's brow furrowed. "What does that mean?"

"It means," Tavriel said, his voice calm but firm, "this shard is a reflection of who we are—and who we were meant to be."

The shard stood in the center of a wide clearing, its surface smooth and reflective. Threads of light and shadow spiraled around it in slow, deliberate patterns, their movements calm yet unyielding.

Kaelion stepped forward, his gaze fixed on the shard. Its resonance hummed softly in the air, the vibrations brushing against his senses like the faintest whisper.

The moment his foot crossed the threshold into the clearing, the air shifted. The threads surrounding the shard unraveled, their energy coiling through the air like serpents. The hum of the shard grew louder, its resonance filling the space with an overwhelming presence.

Kaelion gritted his teeth, his hand tightening on his sword. "Stay alert. This isn't going to be easy."

The threads began to weave into shapes, their forms shifting and flickering like mirages. Faces emerged from the patterns, their features familiar and haunting. Kaelion's breath caught as he recognized them—Selara, Laryn, soldiers from Solaris, villagers from the Broken Step.

"You carry them still," a voice said, calm and resonant.

Kaelion turned toward the shard, his jaw tightening. "They're part of me. I don't let go of what matters."

The shard's light flared, and the threads surged toward the group, their movements sharp and deliberate.

Liora drew her blade, her voice steady. "Then let's prove it."

The battle was unlike anything they had faced before. The threads moved with an eerie precision, their attacks coordinated and unrelenting. Kaelion fought with purpose, each strike cutting through the shifting forms with bursts of light.

Darith moved like a shadow, his blade flashing as he parried another attack. "These things are tougher than they look!"

"They're not things," Tavriel said, his voice steady. "They're reflections—fragments of us, woven into the shard."

Kaelion's movements slowed as the threads shifted, their forms taking on shapes that mirrored the group. A figure stepped forward from the fray, its features an exact reflection of Kaelion's own.

"You fight to mend what you've broken," the reflection said, its voice sharp. "But what will you sacrifice to hold the loom together?"

Kaelion gritted his teeth, his voice firm. "Whatever it takes."

The reflection smiled faintly. "We'll see."

The threads surged toward him, their energy pressing against him like a storm. Kaelion raised his sword, the hum of the Severance Stone vibrating through the blade.

He moved with purpose, his strikes deliberate as he cut through the chaos. The shard's resonance grew louder, its patterns shifting and stabilizing with each movement.

But as the threads began to weave together, Kaelion felt a sharp pull deep within his chest. The shard's energy coiled around him, its resonance pressing against his mind like an unrelenting tide.

"Kaelion!" Tavriel's voice cut through the chaos, sharp and urgent. "The shard is pulling you into the loom. You have to let go!"

Kaelion staggered back, his breath catching in his chest. The threads surrounding the shard coiled tighter, their movements growing more erratic.

"I can't let go," Kaelion said, his voice strained. "If I do, it all falls apart."

Tavriel stepped closer, his blind eyes glowing faintly. "The loom doesn't need a savior, Kaelion. It needs a weaver. Trust the threads to find their place."

Kaelion closed his eyes, the hum of the shard filling his mind. Memories surged to the surface—of Selara's laughter, of Solaris's spires, of every choice that had brought him to this moment.

When he opened his eyes, his gaze was steady. "Then I'll weave."

He stepped forward, his hand brushing against the shard's surface. The world around him shifted, and the void of light and shadow surrounded him once more.

The threads coiled around him, their energy pressing against him with an almost suffocating weight. Kaelion moved with purpose, his strikes precise as he severed the broken threads and wove the stable ones into place.

The shard's resonance shifted, its chaotic hum softening into a steady rhythm. The void stilled, and the threads wove together into a unified whole.

Kaelion opened his eyes to the clearing, the shard standing before him. Its surface was smooth and reflective now, its light glowing with a quiet strength.

Tavriel approached cautiously, his staff glowing faintly. "You've aligned the threads," he said softly. "The loom holds—for now."

Kaelion nodded, his chest heaving as he lowered his hand. "The loom isn't just threads. It's us. And we're not done yet."

Liora stepped forward, her expression thoughtful. "The shards are testing more than our strength. They're testing who we are—and who we choose to be."

Kaelion's gaze turned toward the horizon, where the faint glow of the next shard shimmered in the twilight.

"And we choose to keep going."

# Chapter Twenty-One: The Loom's Threads Fray

The journey to the next shard felt heavier than the others. Each step seemed to pull against them, the very air growing dense with the weight of unseen threads that resisted their movements. The skies above the Twilight Marches shifted into ominous hues, streaked with turbulent clouds that churned like liquid dusk.

Kaelion led the group in silence, his thoughts swirling as the weight of the shard's trials pressed heavily on his chest. They were growing stronger—more complex, more dangerous. The closer they came to the loom's core, the harder it fought to resist mending.

Liora walked alongside him, her expression pensive. The glow of the last shard still lingered faintly on her armor, a reminder of the tenuous trust she had reclaimed.

"You've been quiet," she said softly, breaking the silence.

Kaelion glanced at her, his jaw tightening. "I've been thinking."

"About the shards?"

"About what happens when we finish this," Kaelion admitted, his voice low. "If we finish this."

Liora nodded, her gaze distant. "That's the trick, isn't it? Fixing the loom won't erase what we've done—or what we've lost."

Kaelion's grip on his sword tightened. "No. But maybe it'll mean something."

The group crested a ridge, and the next shard came into view. It stood at the heart of a windswept expanse, its surface fractured and jagged. Threads of light and shadow spiraled around it in violent patterns, their movements erratic and frenzied.

The air hummed with the shard's resonance, a discordant vibration that rippled through the ground like a drumbeat. The grass beneath their feet wilted as they approached, the shard's energy leeching life from the landscape.

Darith let out a low whistle, his tone tinged with unease. "This one's worse than the last."

"It's more than unstable," Tavriel said, his blind eyes narrowing. "The threads are breaking—tearing away from the loom entirely."

Kaelion's chest tightened as he stepped closer, the shard's pull growing stronger with each step. "Then we don't have time to waste."

The ground trembled as they entered the shard's radius, the threads surrounding it unraveling in bursts of chaotic energy. The air grew colder, the shard's resonance pressing against them like an unrelenting tide.

Figures emerged from the fray, their forms twisted and jagged. They moved with erratic precision, their bodies flickering like mirages. Kaelion drew his sword, his voice sharp. "Shard-forged."

Liora stepped forward, her blade gleaming faintly. "And there's more of them this time."

The shard-forged attacked without hesitation, their movements swift and brutal. Kaelion met the first wave head-on, his strikes deliberate as he cut through their chaotic forms. Each blow sent ripples through the air, the shard's resonance growing louder with every moment.

Darith fought at his side, his strikes quick and precise. "These things are getting stronger!"

"They're feeding off the shard's instability," Tavriel said, his voice strained. "The longer we take, the worse it will get."

Kaelion's movements slowed as the shard's resonance shifted, its energy surging in violent waves. The threads surrounding it coiled and lashed out, their movements growing faster and more erratic.

He fought his way toward the shard, his breath heavy as he pushed through the chaos. Each step forward felt like a battle in itself, the shard's pull growing stronger with every moment.

The shard-forged converged on him, their attacks relentless. Kaelion's jaw tightened as he raised his sword, his voice steady. "Keep them off me!"

Liora and Darith moved to his sides, their blades flashing as they held the line. Tavriel stood at the edge of the fray, his staff glowing faintly as he chanted a low incantation. The air around him shimmered, a web of shadowlight spreading outward to disrupt the shard-forged's resonance.

"Kaelion!" Tavriel's voice cut through the chaos. "The threads are pulling apart. You have to act now!"

Kaelion reached the base of the shard, its energy crackling against his skin. The threads surrounding it spiraled in chaotic patterns, their movements erratic and unstable.

He raised his hand, his fingers brushing against the shard's surface. The world shifted.

Kaelion found himself standing in a void of swirling light and shadow, the shard's core glowing faintly before him. The threads surrounding it were frayed and broken, their movements clashing and unraveling in chaotic bursts.

A voice echoed through the void, sharp and resonant. "The loom unravels. The weave collapses. What will you sever to hold it together?"

Kaelion's chest tightened as the threads began to weave into shapes—familiar faces and places that flickered like fading memories. Selara's laughter echoed faintly, followed by the cries of the innocents he had failed to save.

"I'll sever what I must," Kaelion said quietly, his voice steady. "But I won't lose myself."

The threads surged toward him, their energy pressing against him like a storm. Kaelion moved with purpose, his strikes precise as he cut through the chaos, severing the broken threads and weaving the stable ones into place.

The shard's resonance shifted, its chaotic hum softening into a steady rhythm. The void stilled, the threads weaving together into intricate patterns that flickered with the promise of unity.

Kaelion stepped back, his chest heaving as the shard's light flared, filling the void with blinding brilliance.

Kaelion opened his eyes to the battlefield, the shard standing before him. Its surface was smooth and steady now, its light glowing with a quiet strength.

Liora approached cautiously, her blade still in hand. "That was close," she said, her voice edged with relief.

Tavriel stepped forward, his expression calm but weary. "The threads are holding. But the loom isn't whole yet."

Kaelion nodded, his gaze turning toward the horizon. The faint glow of the next shard shimmered in the distance, a silent reminder of the trials yet to come.

"And we're not done yet."

# Chapter Twenty-Two: The Bound Loom

The journey to the next shard was oppressively quiet. The faint glow of the shard ahead cast the landscape in eerie hues of silver and black, illuminating jagged cliffs and sharp outcroppings that loomed like silent sentinels. The air itself felt heavier, pressing down on the group with an almost suffocating intensity.

Kaelion led the way, his gaze fixed on the distant shard. Its resonance pulsed faintly through the air, a low, rhythmic hum that seemed to mirror his own heartbeat.

"This isn't like the others," Tavriel said quietly, his blind eyes narrowing as his staff tapped against the rocky ground. "The shard's threads are bound—restrained. Something is holding them back."

Darith frowned, his tone edged with unease. "Is that a good thing or a bad thing?"

Tavriel's grip on his staff tightened. "Both. If the threads are bound, they're stable. But if we disturb them... the entire loom could backlash."

Kaelion stopped at the edge of a narrow ravine, his jaw tightening as he studied the path ahead. "Then we'll move carefully. No mistakes."

The ravine narrowed as they descended, its steep walls casting long shadows that twisted and shifted with the shard's faint light. The ground beneath their feet was smooth and polished, as though shaped by deliberate hands.

Liora ran her fingers along the stone, her brow furrowing. "This place was made for something. It's not natural."

"It's a binding chamber," Tavriel said, his voice reverent. "An ancient structure built to contain the Axis's energy when it fractured. The shard is at its heart."

Darith glanced around, his hand resting on the hilt of his blade. "And let me guess—whatever built this didn't leave it unguarded."

Kaelion nodded, his expression grim. "Stay alert. We don't know what we're walking into."

The chamber at the end of the ravine was vast and circular, its walls carved with intricate patterns that shimmered faintly in the shard's light. At its center stood the shard, its surface smooth and reflective. Threads of light and shadow coiled around it like chains, their movements slow and deliberate.

The shard's resonance filled the chamber, its rhythmic hum vibrating through the air like a heartbeat. Kaelion stepped forward, his gaze fixed on the shard.

"The threads are bound," Tavriel said softly, his voice tinged with awe. "This shard isn't just unstable—it's locked in place."

Kaelion glanced at him, his brow furrowing. "Can we stabilize it?"

Tavriel hesitated, his blind eyes narrowing. "We can. But unlocking the threads will release all of its stored energy. The loom won't just resist—it'll lash out."

The air in the chamber shifted, and the threads surrounding the shard began to stir. The rhythmic hum of its resonance grew louder, its vibrations pressing against their senses like an unrelenting tide.

Kaelion drew his sword, his voice steady. "We don't have a choice. Tavriel, guide the threads. The rest of us will hold the line."

As if in response, the shard's energy flared, and the chains of light and shadow unravelled. The ground trembled beneath their feet as the threads surged outward, coalescing into shifting forms that moved with an unnatural grace.

Liora drew her blade, her stance steady. "Here we go again."

The figures attacked with brutal precision, their movements swift and unrelenting. Kaelion met the first wave head-on, his strikes deliberate as he cut through their chaotic forms. Each blow sent ripples through the air, the shard's resonance growing louder with every moment.

Tavriel stood at the edge of the fray, his staff planted firmly in the ground. The air around him shimmered as he chanted a low, rhythmic incantation, the threads surrounding the shard responding to his movements.

"The shard's energy is tied to this place," he called out, his voice strained. "The chains were holding it together. Without them, the loom is unraveling faster."

Kaelion parried another attack, his movements deliberate. "Then lock it back in place!"

"I can't!" Tavriel shouted, his voice sharp. "The threads are already breaking. We have to weave them into the loom—or lose them completely."

Kaelion's jaw tightened as he fought his way toward the shard, his breath heavy as the shard's energy pressed against him like a storm.

He reached the base of the shard, its surface glowing with an intense, fractured light. The threads surrounding it lashed out, their movements erratic and violent. Kaelion raised his hand, his fingers brushing against the shard's surface.

The world shifted.

Kaelion stood in a void of swirling light and shadow, the shard's core glowing faintly before him. The threads surrounding it were tangled and frayed, their movements clashing and unraveling in chaotic bursts.

A voice echoed through the void, calm and resonant. "The loom's bonds are breaking. What will you bind to hold it together?"

Kaelion's chest tightened as the threads began to weave into shapes. Selara appeared before him, her violet eyes glimmering with quiet sorrow. Behind her, the faces of his companions and the countless lives he had touched flickered in and out of focus.

"You can't hold us all," Selara said softly, her voice steady. "You have to let go."

Kaelion's breath caught in his chest. "I can't. If I let go, the loom falls apart."

Selara stepped closer, her gaze unwavering. "The loom doesn't need control, Kaelion. It needs trust."

Kaelion closed his eyes, the hum of the shard filling his mind. Memories surged to the surface—of battles fought and lost, of choices made and regretted. Each memory was a thread, fragile and frayed, woven into the fabric of his purpose.

When he opened his eyes, his gaze was steady. "I'll trust the loom."

He stepped forward, his hand brushing against the shard's core. The threads coiled around him, their energy pressing against him with an almost suffocating weight. Kaelion moved with purpose, his strikes deliberate as he severed the broken threads and wove the stable ones into place.

The shard's resonance shifted, its chaotic hum softening into a steady rhythm. The void stilled, the threads weaving together into intricate patterns that flickered with the promise of unity.

Kaelion opened his eyes to the chamber, the shard standing before him. Its surface was smooth and reflective now, its light glowing with a quiet strength.

Tavriel approached cautiously, his staff glowing faintly. "The threads are bound again," he said softly. "The loom holds—for now."

Kaelion nodded, his chest heaving as he lowered his hand. "It's not just about weaving. It's about trust."

Liora stepped forward, her expression thoughtful. "The shards are teaching us more than we realize."

Kaelion's gaze turned toward the horizon, where the faint glow of the next shard shimmered in the distance.

"And we're not done yet."

# Chapter Twenty-Three: The Loom's Whisper

The night had fallen, though in the Twilight Marches, it felt less like darkness and more like a deepening of the eternal dusk. The group trudged across an expanse of rolling hills, the grass beneath their feet glowing faintly as if imbued with the stars themselves. The air was heavy with silence, broken only by the faint whispers of the wind that carried a strange, almost sentient hum.

Kaelion's steps slowed as the glow of the next shard came into view. Its light was soft, pulsing in gentle waves that seemed to ripple outward like the beating of a heart. Unlike the others, its presence didn't feel oppressive—it was calm, almost inviting.

Darith adjusted his sword on his shoulder, his voice breaking the quiet. "That's not right. The shards have never felt like this."

Tavriel tilted his head, his expression unreadable. "This shard is different. Its threads are woven deeply into the loom—it carries the whispers of the Axis itself."

Kaelion stopped at the crest of a hill, his gaze fixed on the shard's faint glow. "Whispers?"

Tavriel nodded slowly. "The loom is trying to speak to us. But whether it's a warning or a plea remains to be seen."

The shard was nestled at the base of a shallow valley, its surface smooth and unbroken. Threads of light and shadow spiraled gently around it, their movements deliberate and unhurried. The air in the valley was cool, carrying the faint scent of wildflowers and earth.

Kaelion descended cautiously, his hand resting on the hilt of his sword. The shard's resonance was soft, its vibrations weaving through the air in a melody that was both haunting and beautiful.

"This isn't right," Liora said, her voice low. "It's too quiet."

"It's not quiet," Tavriel corrected, his staff glowing faintly. "The shard is listening."

Kaelion glanced at him, his jaw tightening. "Listening for what?"

"For us," Tavriel said simply.

The air shifted as they entered the shard's radius, its resonance growing louder. The threads surrounding it moved with purpose now, their patterns weaving into intricate shapes that flickered like fleeting memories.

Kaelion stopped a few paces from the shard, his gaze fixed on its surface. For a moment, he thought he saw his own reflection staring back at him, but it shifted—a flicker of Selara's face, then Tavriel's, then Liora's.

"It's showing us," Liora said softly, her voice edged with unease. "It's reflecting what it sees in us."

Tavriel stepped forward, his staff planted firmly in the ground. "The shard carries the Axis's whispers. It holds the loom's truths—and its lies."

Kaelion's chest tightened as the shard's light flared, and the threads spiraled outward, coiling through the air like living things.

The threads began to weave into shapes, their forms flickering and shifting like mirages. Faces appeared before them—Selara, Darith's lost comrades, the villagers Kaelion had failed to save. Their gazes were steady, their voices silent but deafening.

Kaelion stepped forward, his voice sharp. "What do you want from us?"

The shard pulsed, and the voices came, overlapping and indistinct. "The loom is breaking. The threads are fraying. What will you weave to hold it together?"

Kaelion's jaw tightened. "Whatever it takes."

The voices grew louder, their tones shifting from sorrowful to accusing. "You carry what is broken. You weave what is undone. But what will you leave behind?"

The ground trembled, and the threads surrounding the shard unraveled, their energy surging outward in bursts of light and shadow. Figures emerged from the chaos, their forms jagged and indistinct.

Kaelion raised his sword, his voice steady. "Hold the line. Don't let them reach the shard."

The figures attacked with brutal precision, their movements swift and unrelenting. Kaelion met the first wave head-on, his strikes cutting through their forms with bursts of light. Each blow sent ripples through the air, the shard's resonance vibrating in response.

Darith fought beside him, his strikes quick and decisive. "These things again? Don't they ever get tired of this?"

"They're not the same," Tavriel called out, his voice sharp. "These are echoes—reflections of us. They're testing our threads."

Kaelion's movements slowed as the figures shifted, their forms taking on familiar shapes. One of them stepped forward, its features an exact reflection of him.

"You weave to fix what you've broken," the reflection said, its voice sharp. "But what will you sever to make it whole?"

Kaelion's chest tightened as he raised his sword. "I'll sever what I must. But I won't lose myself."

The battle raged on, the figures pressing closer to the shard. Tavriel stood at its edge, his staff glowing as he chanted a low incantation. The air around him shimmered, a web of shadowlight spreading outward to disrupt the figures' resonance.

"They're tied to the shard's energy," Tavriel said, his voice strained. "If we don't stabilize it, they won't stop."

Kaelion fought his way toward the shard, his breath heavy as the chaotic energy pressed against him. Each step forward felt heavier, the shard's resonance pulling at him with every moment.

He reached the base of the shard, its surface glowing with a calm, steady light. The threads surrounding it coiled and lashed out, their movements deliberate but unrelenting. Kaelion raised his hand, his fingers brushing against the shard's surface.

The world shifted.

Kaelion stood in a void of swirling light and shadow, the shard's core glowing faintly before him. The threads surrounding it were tangled and frayed, their movements clashing and unraveling in chaotic bursts.

A voice echoed through the void, calm and resonant. "The loom whispers. The threads speak. What will you hear—and what will you leave unheard?"

Kaelion's chest tightened as the threads began to weave into shapes. Memories flickered before him—Selara's laughter, Solaris's spires, the faces of those he had failed to save.

"I'll hear what I must," Kaelion said quietly, his voice steady. "But I won't let it break me."

The threads surged toward him, their energy pressing against him like a storm. Kaelion moved with purpose, his strikes deliberate as he severed the broken threads and wove the stable ones into place.

The shard's resonance shifted, its melodic hum softening into a steady rhythm. The void stilled, the threads weaving together into intricate patterns that flickered with the promise of unity.

Kaelion opened his eyes to the clearing, the shard standing before him. Its surface was smooth and reflective now, its light glowing with a quiet strength.

Tavriel approached cautiously, his staff glowing faintly. "The loom whispers," he said softly. "And it waits for your answer."

Kaelion nodded, his chest heaving as he lowered his hand. "Then we keep weaving."

Liora stepped forward, her gaze thoughtful. "The shards are teaching us more than just balance. They're teaching us how to listen."

Kaelion's gaze turned toward the horizon, where the faint glow of the next shard shimmered in the distance.

"And we're not done yet."

# Chapter Twenty-Four: The Shard of Reckoning

The landscape stretched into endless gray, a featureless expanse that seemed to shift and ripple like water underfoot. The sky above mirrored the ground, a seamless gradient of light and shadow that offered no horizon, no sense of direction. The shard's glow was distant but unyielding, its resonance a low, relentless hum that vibrated through the group's bones.

"This is... unnatural," Darith muttered, his hand resting on the hilt of his blade. "Feels like the world's unraveling around us."

"It is," Tavriel said softly, his blind eyes narrowing as his staff tapped lightly against the ground. "We're nearing the loom's core. The threads are thinner here, more fragile. The wrong step could pull the entire weave apart."

Kaelion paused, his gaze fixed on the shard's faint glow in the distance. Its light pulsed in time with the hum of its resonance, a rhythm that seemed to echo in his own chest.

"We don't have time to tread carefully," Kaelion said, his voice firm. "The loom's holding together by a thread. If we don't reach the shard soon, there won't be anything left to save."

The group moved cautiously across the shifting expanse, the ground beneath their feet rippling with every step. The shard's glow grew brighter as they approached, its resonance intensifying until it was almost deafening.

Kaelion stopped at the edge of a vast circular basin, its walls carved with intricate patterns that shimmered faintly in the shard's light. The shard stood at its center, its surface fractured and jagged. Threads of light and shadow spiraled around it, their movements chaotic and violent.

"The shard's resonance is tearing at the loom," Tavriel said, his voice edged with unease. "If we stabilize it, the energy release could be catastrophic."

"And if we don't?" Liora asked, her tone sharp.

Tavriel's grip on his staff tightened. "Then the loom collapses. Everything we've fought for will unravel."

Kaelion stepped forward, his jaw tightening. "Then we stabilize it. No matter the cost."

The ground trembled as they entered the basin, the shard's energy pressing against them like an unrelenting tide. The air grew colder, the shard's chaotic resonance vibrating through their bodies with every step.

Kaelion raised his sword, his voice steady. "Stay sharp. The shard won't let us take it without a fight."

As if in response, the threads surrounding the shard unraveled, their energy coiling through the air like serpents. Figures emerged from the chaos, their forms jagged and shifting. Unlike the shard-forged they had faced before, these creatures moved with deliberate purpose, their gazes fixed on the group with an almost sentient awareness.

"They're different," Darith said, his voice tight. "Smarter."

"They're echoes of the core," Tavriel said, his voice calm but firm. "They carry the Axis's will. And they won't stop until we do."

The battle erupted in a storm of light and shadow. Kaelion met the first wave head-on, his strikes cutting through the figures with bursts of radiant energy. Each blow sent ripples through the air, the shard's resonance growing louder with every moment.

Liora fought beside him, her blade flashing as she parried another attack. The figures moved with uncanny precision, their movements coordinated and unrelenting.

Darith circled the fray, his strikes quick and decisive. "These things are adapting. Every time we take one down, they come back stronger."

"They're feeding off the shard's energy," Tavriel called out, his staff glowing faintly as he chanted a low incantation. "If we don't stabilize it soon, they'll overwhelm us."

Kaelion pushed forward, his breath heavy as he fought his way toward the shard. The ground beneath his feet cracked and splintered, threads of light and shadow spiraling upward to block his path.

He raised his sword, the hum of the Severance Stone vibrating through the blade. "Tavriel! Can you guide the threads?"

Tavriel's voice was sharp. "Not while the shard is this unstable. You have to get closer."

Kaelion gritted his teeth, his movements deliberate as he cut through the chaos. The shard loomed before him, its surface glowing with a violent, fractured light that pulsed in time with its resonance.

He reached the base of the shard, the storm of energy surrounding it crackling against his skin. The threads spiraling around it lashed out, their movements erratic and unpredictable.

Kaelion raised his hand, his fingers brushing against the shard's surface.

The world shifted.

Kaelion stood in a void of swirling light and shadow, the shard's core glowing faintly before him. The threads surrounding it were tangled and broken, their movements clashing and unraveling in chaotic bursts.

A voice echoed through the void, calm and resonant. "The loom frays. The threads unravel. What will you weave to make it whole?"

Kaelion's chest tightened as the threads began to weave into shapes. Faces flickered before him—Selara, Darith, Liora, Tavriel. Their gazes were steady, their voices silent but heavy with expectation.

"I'll weave what's needed," Kaelion said quietly, his voice steady. "But I won't let it destroy me."

The threads surged toward him, their energy pressing against him like a storm. Kaelion moved with purpose, his strikes deliberate as he severed the broken threads and wove the stable ones into place.

The shard's resonance shifted, its chaotic hum softening into a steady rhythm. The void stilled, the threads weaving together into intricate patterns that flickered with the promise of unity.

Kaelion opened his eyes to the basin, the shard standing before him. Its surface was smooth and reflective now, its light glowing with a quiet strength.

The figures surrounding them dissolved into threads of light and shadow, their energy spiraling back toward the shard's core. The air grew still, the shard's resonance fading into a quiet hum.

Tavriel approached cautiously, his staff glowing faintly. "The threads are holding. The loom remains intact."

Kaelion nodded, his chest heaving as he lowered his sword. "But it's not finished yet."

Liora stepped forward, her expression weary but resolute. "Then we keep going. We're not stopping now."

Kaelion's gaze turned toward the horizon, where the faint glow of the next shard shimmered in the distance.

"And we're not done yet."

# Chapter Twenty-Five: The Woven Path

The horizon was fractured—jagged streaks of light and shadow split the sky like scars. The ground beneath the group's feet was hard and unyielding, made of a dull, crystalline substance that resonated faintly with each step. The air was unnaturally still, as if the world itself was holding its breath.

Kaelion walked at the front, his gaze fixed on the glow of the next shard ahead. It shimmered faintly in the distance, its resonance low and almost melodic. But there was something unnatural about its pull—something deliberate, as though it was leading them into its own carefully laid snare.

"This path isn't random," Tavriel said, his blind eyes narrowing as his staff tapped against the ground. "The threads are guiding us toward something. Something deliberate."

Darith glanced around, his hand resting on the hilt of his blade. "Do we know if that's a good thing or a bad thing?"

"It's neither," Tavriel said quietly. "The loom doesn't think in terms of good or bad. It only seeks balance."

"And if balance means breaking us in the process?" Liora asked, her tone sharp.

Tavriel didn't answer.

The shard's resonance grew stronger as they approached, its hum vibrating through the crystalline ground beneath their feet. The jagged landscape seemed to shift subtly, its sharp edges catching and reflecting the shard's light in patterns that rippled like water.

Kaelion slowed his pace as the shard came into view. It was nestled in the center of a vast expanse, its surface smooth and reflective. Threads of light and shadow spiraled around it in intricate patterns, their movements deliberate and methodical.

"It's different," Liora said softly, her voice edged with unease.

"It's waiting," Tavriel replied, his tone calm but tense. "This shard isn't unraveling. It's testing us."

Kaelion tightened his grip on his sword, his jaw setting. "Then we'll face the test. Together."

The ground trembled as they stepped into the shard's radius, the threads surrounding it unraveling and coiling outward like living things. The shard's resonance grew louder, its vibrations pressing against them like an invisible tide.

Kaelion raised his sword, his voice steady. "Be ready. This won't be like the others."

The threads began to weave into shapes, their movements deliberate and precise. Figures emerged from the fray, their forms sharp and angular, their features eerily familiar.

Kaelion's chest tightened as one of the figures stepped forward. It was him—or rather, a reflection of him, its gaze steady and unyielding.

"You weave to mend the loom," the reflection said, its voice calm and resonant. "But what will you sever to finish the pattern?"

Kaelion gritted his teeth, his sword raised. "I've heard this before. I'll sever what I must—but I won't lose myself."

The reflection smiled faintly. "Then prove it."

The figures attacked in unison, their movements swift and coordinated. Kaelion met the first wave head-on, his strikes cutting through their forms with bursts of radiant energy. Each blow sent ripples through the air, the shard's resonance growing louder with every moment.

Liora fought beside him, her blade flashing as she parried another attack. The figures moved with precision, their strikes deliberate and unrelenting.

"These aren't just echoes," she said sharply. "They're part of the shard itself. They're testing the weave."

Darith circled the fray, his strikes quick and decisive. "They're learning as they fight. The longer this goes on, the harder they'll get to kill."

"Then we don't give them time," Kaelion said, his voice firm.

He pushed forward, his movements deliberate as he fought his way toward the shard. The figures surrounding it converged on him, their attacks growing faster and more coordinated. Kaelion's breath was heavy as he parried another strike, the shard's resonance pressing against him like an unrelenting tide.

"Tavriel!" Kaelion shouted over the din. "Can you stabilize the threads?"

Tavriel stood at the edge of the fray, his staff glowing faintly. "Not while they're bound to the shard. You have to sever them first!"

Kaelion gritted his teeth, his gaze fixed on the shard. "Then I'll do it myself."

He reached the base of the shard, its surface glowing with a calm, steady light. The threads surrounding it coiled and lashed out, their movements deliberate but unrelenting.

Kaelion raised his hand, his fingers brushing against the shard's surface.

The world shifted.

Kaelion stood in a void of swirling light and shadow, the shard's core glowing faintly before him. The threads surrounding it were tangled and broken, their movements clashing and unraveling in chaotic bursts.

A voice echoed through the void, calm and resonant. "The loom holds its secrets. The threads whisper their truths. Will you listen—or will you sever them?"

Kaelion's chest tightened as the threads began to weave into shapes. Memories flickered before him—Selara's laughter, Darith's loss, Liora's redemption. Each thread was a choice, fragile and fleeting.

"I'll listen," Kaelion said quietly, his voice steady. "But I'll choose what to weave."

The threads surged toward him, their energy pressing against him like a storm. Kaelion moved with purpose, his strikes deliberate as he severed the broken threads and wove the stable ones into place.

The shard's resonance shifted, its melodic hum softening into a steady rhythm. The void stilled, the threads weaving together into intricate patterns that flickered with the promise of unity.

Kaelion opened his eyes to the battlefield, the shard standing before him. Its surface was smooth and reflective now, its light glowing with a quiet strength.

The figures surrounding them dissolved into threads of light and shadow, their energy spiraling back toward the shard's core. The air grew still, the shard's resonance fading into a quiet hum.

Tavriel approached cautiously, his staff glowing faintly. "The threads are holding. The loom remains intact—for now."

Kaelion nodded, his chest heaving as he lowered his sword. "But the loom isn't finished yet."

Liora stepped forward, her expression weary but resolute. "Then we keep going. We're not stopping now."

Kaelion's gaze turned toward the horizon, where the faint glow of the next shard shimmered in the distance.

"And we're not done yet."

# Chapter Twenty-Six: The Broken Weave

The horizon shifted with a strange, distorted light, like a mirage fractured into jagged shards. The landscape around the group was sparse and barren, its once-familiar twilight hues replaced with a strange gradient of silvery white and shadowy black. Every step forward seemed heavier, as if the weight of the loom itself pressed against them.

Kaelion gritted his teeth as the glow of the next shard came into view. It flickered erratically, its resonance jagged and sharp, slicing through the still air like the toll of a broken bell.

"This one isn't just unstable," Tavriel said, his blind eyes narrowing as he leaned on his staff. "The threads here are completely severed. The shard is... disconnected."

Darith frowned, his voice edged with unease. "Disconnected from what?"

"The loom," Tavriel said softly. "If we don't reweave it, the entire structure will collapse."

Kaelion tightened his grip on his sword, his gaze fixed on the distant shard. "Then we have no choice. We fix it, or the loom breaks for good."

The shard stood at the heart of a massive crater, its surface cracked and fragmented. Unlike the others, its glow was faint and erratic, its resonance a discordant hum that sent sharp vibrations through the ground.

Kaelion stopped at the crater's edge, his jaw tightening as he studied the shard. Threads of light and shadow spiraled chaotically around it, their movements erratic and violent. The energy radiating from the shard felt raw and unrestrained, like an open wound in the fabric of reality.

"This isn't going to be like the others," Liora said, her voice steady but tense. "It's not just unstable—it's broken."

Kaelion nodded, his gaze unwavering. "Then we'll mend it. No matter what it takes."

The group descended into the crater, the shard's chaotic energy pressing against them with each step. The air grew colder, the shard's resonance growing louder until it was almost deafening.

As they reached the shard's radius, the ground trembled, and the threads surrounding it unraveled. Figures emerged from the chaos, their forms jagged and indistinct. Unlike the shard-forged they had faced before, these figures seemed fractured, their movements erratic and unpredictable.

"They're not whole," Darith said, his tone laced with unease. "They're like the shard—broken."

"And just as dangerous," Liora said sharply, her blade flashing as she took a defensive stance.

Kaelion raised his sword, his voice firm. "Hold the line. We need to stabilize the shard."

The battle erupted in a storm of light and shadow. Kaelion met the first wave head-on, his strikes cutting through the fractured figures with bursts of radiant energy. Each blow sent ripples through the air, the shard's resonance growing louder with every moment.

Liora fought beside him, her movements deliberate and precise. The fractured figures moved erratically, their attacks unpredictable and relentless.

"These things are barely holding together," Darith called out, his strikes quick and decisive. "But that makes them harder to predict!"

"They're tied to the shard," Tavriel said, his staff glowing faintly as he chanted a low incantation. "If we don't stabilize it, they'll keep coming."

Kaelion pushed forward, his movements deliberate as he fought his way toward the shard. The ground beneath his feet cracked and splintered, threads of light and shadow spiraling upward to block his path.

He reached the base of the shard, its surface glowing faintly. The threads surrounding it coiled and lashed out, their movements erratic and violent. Kaelion raised his hand, his fingers brushing against the shard's surface.

The world shifted.

Kaelion stood in a void of swirling light and shadow, the shard's core glowing faintly before him. The threads surrounding it were tangled and broken, their movements clashing and unraveling in chaotic bursts.

A voice echoed through the void, calm and resonant. "The loom unravels. The weave frays. What will you sacrifice to mend what is broken?"

Kaelion's chest tightened as the threads began to weave into shapes. Memories flickered before him—Selara's smile, the laughter of comrades long gone, the faces of those he had failed to save.

"I'll sacrifice what's needed," Kaelion said quietly, his voice steady. "But I won't let it break me."

The threads surged toward him, their energy pressing against him like a storm. Kaelion moved with purpose, his strikes deliberate as he severed the broken threads and wove the stable ones into place.

The shard's resonance shifted, its chaotic hum softening into a steady rhythm. The void stilled, the threads weaving together into intricate patterns that flickered with the promise of unity.

Kaelion opened his eyes to the battlefield, the shard standing before him. Its surface was smooth and reflective now, its light glowing with a quiet strength.

The fractured figures surrounding them dissolved into threads of light and shadow, their energy spiraling back toward the shard's core. The air grew still, the shard's resonance fading into a quiet hum.

Tavriel approached cautiously, his staff glowing faintly. "The threads are reconnected. The shard is whole again."

Kaelion nodded, his chest heaving as he lowered his sword. "But the loom still isn't finished."

Liora stepped forward, her expression weary but resolute. "We're running out of time. The threads are fraying faster than we can weave them."

Kaelion's gaze turned toward the horizon, where the faint glow of the next shard shimmered in the distance.

"Then we keep moving. We finish this."

# Chapter Twenty-Seven: The Axis Fractures

The wind whipped through the jagged landscape, carrying with it a discordant hum that set the group's nerves on edge. The shard ahead shimmered with violent, erratic light, its resonance splintering into a chaotic cacophony.

Kaelion's steps slowed as the shard came into full view. It was unlike any they had encountered before. Its surface was cracked, and from those fractures poured streams of raw energy—light and shadow interwoven yet tearing at each other in a ceaseless struggle. The threads surrounding it lashed out violently, like serpents striking at invisible foes.

"This isn't just unstable," Liora said, her voice tight with unease. "It's ripping itself apart."

Tavriel's blind eyes glimmered faintly, his expression grim. "The shard is rejecting the loom. The Axis is fighting back, resisting its own mending."

"Why?" Darith asked, his tone sharp. "What could it possibly gain by tearing itself to pieces?"

Tavriel turned his head toward Kaelion. "Because we're forcing it. The Axis is alive, Kaelion. It doesn't just respond to balance—it demands intention. It demands understanding."

Kaelion's grip on his sword tightened. His voice was low but firm. "Then we make it understand."

The shard's resonance grew louder as they approached, its chaotic vibrations pressing against them with an almost suffocating weight. The ground beneath their feet cracked and splintered, jagged threads of light and shadow spiraling upward in erratic bursts.

Kaelion stopped just short of the shard's radius, his gaze fixed on its fractured surface. The energy pouring from it was raw and unrelenting, its presence almost overwhelming.

"This one won't let us in without a fight," Liora said, her blade already drawn.

Darith glanced around, his hand resting on his hilt. "And I don't think it's going to wait for us to start it."

As if on cue, the threads surrounding the shard began to weave into forms, their movements sharp and deliberate. Figures emerged from the chaos, their bodies fractured and jagged, their eyes glowing with the shard's violent light.

"They're not echoes," Tavriel said, his voice tense. "They're manifestations of the Axis itself."

Kaelion raised his sword, his voice steady. "Then we face them together."

The battle erupted in a storm of light and shadow. The manifestations moved with an unnatural grace, their attacks swift and precise. Kaelion met the first wave head-on, his strikes cutting through their forms with bursts of radiant energy. Each blow sent ripples through the air, the shard's resonance growing louder with every moment.

Darith fought beside him, his movements quick and deliberate. "These things are smarter than the others. They're adapting to us."

"They're not just defending the shard," Liora said sharply, her blade flashing as she parried another attack. "They're testing us."

Kaelion pushed forward, his breath heavy as he fought his way toward the shard. The manifestations pressed closer, their attacks relentless. Each step forward felt heavier, the shard's energy pulling at him with every moment.

He reached the base of the shard, its surface glowing with violent, fractured light. The threads surrounding it coiled and lashed out, their movements erratic and unpredictable.

Kaelion raised his hand, his fingers brushing against the shard's surface.

The world shifted.

Kaelion stood in a void of swirling light and shadow, the shard's core glowing faintly before him. The threads surrounding it were tangled and broken, their movements clashing and unraveling in chaotic bursts.

A voice echoed through the void, calm but resonant. "The Axis resists. The loom fractures. What will you weave to restore it?"

Kaelion's chest tightened as the threads began to weave into shapes. Selara's face flickered before him, her violet eyes filled with quiet sorrow. Behind her, Tavriel, Liora, and Darith appeared, their gazes steady but heavy with expectation.

"I'll weave what's needed," Kaelion said quietly, his voice steady. "But I won't lose myself."

The threads surged toward him, their energy pressing against him like a storm. Memories surfaced unbidden—of battles fought and lost, of choices made and regretted. Each memory was a thread, fragile and frayed, waiting to be woven into the loom.

Kaelion closed his eyes, his breath steady. "You want intention? Then here it is."

He moved with purpose, his strikes deliberate as he severed the broken threads and wove the stable ones into place. The shard's resonance shifted, its chaotic hum softening into a steady rhythm.

The void stilled, the threads weaving together into intricate patterns that flickered with the promise of unity.

Kaelion opened his eyes to the battlefield, the shard standing before him. Its surface was smooth and reflective now, its light glowing with a quiet strength.

The manifestations dissolved into threads of light and shadow, their energy spiraling back toward the shard's core. The air grew still, the shard's resonance fading into a quiet hum.

Tavriel approached cautiously, his staff glowing faintly. "The threads are holding. The loom remains intact—for now."

Kaelion nodded, his chest heaving as he lowered his sword. "But it's not finished yet."

Liora stepped forward, her expression weary but resolute. "We're running out of time. The threads are fraying faster than we can weave them."

Kaelion's gaze turned toward the horizon, where the faint glow of the next shard shimmered in the distance.

"Then we keep moving. We finish this."

# Chapter Twenty-Eight: The Loom Unseen

The ground shifted beneath their feet as they approached the next shard, no longer solid but fluid like molten glass. The silvery-black surface rippled with each step, mirroring their movements in unsettling clarity. Overhead, the twilight sky bled into a kaleidoscope of fractured colors, each streak of light flickering like a candle about to be snuffed out.

"This place feels... wrong," Darith muttered, his tone edged with unease.

"It's not the shard," Tavriel said softly, his blind eyes narrowing. "It's the loom itself. We're too close to the core. The threads are unraveling faster than we can mend them."

Kaelion stopped, his gaze fixed on the shard ahead. It floated above the rippling ground, its surface fractured and jagged. Unlike the others, this shard radiated a blinding intensity, its resonance a high-pitched, unrelenting wail that set his teeth on edge.

"This one is different," Kaelion said, his voice low. "It's... exposed."

"It's raw," Tavriel said, his expression grim. "A piece of the Axis that was never meant to be touched."

Liora drew her blade, her stance steady. "Then we'd better not touch it for long."

The shard's resonance grew louder as they approached, its vibrations rippling through the fluid ground beneath their feet.

Threads of light and shadow spiraled chaotically around it, their movements sharp and deliberate. The air was heavy with energy, each breath feeling like an effort to draw through an unseen barrier.

Kaelion tightened his grip on his sword, his jaw set. "Be ready. This one's going to fight us harder than the others."

The moment they stepped into the shard's radius, the ground beneath them erupted. Threads surged upward like jagged spires, forming a cage of light and shadow around the shard. The high-pitched wail of its resonance grew louder, nearly deafening.

"What's it doing?" Liora shouted, her voice barely audible over the noise.

"It's defending itself," Tavriel called back, his staff glowing faintly. "The shard knows we're here to change it—and it's resisting with everything it has."

Kaelion raised his sword, his voice steady despite the chaos. "Then we push through."

Figures emerged from the spiraling threads, their forms sharp and angular, their movements quick and coordinated. Unlike the fractured manifestations they had faced before, these were whole—perfectly formed reflections of the group, each one radiating the shard's raw energy.

Kaelion's chest tightened as his own reflection stepped forward, its gaze steady and unyielding. "You weave to mend," the reflection said, its voice an exact match for his own. "But what will you sacrifice to make the loom whole?"

Kaelion gritted his teeth, his sword raised. "I'll sacrifice what's needed. But I won't lose myself."

The reflection smiled faintly. "Then let us see."

The battle began with brutal intensity. The mirrored figures moved with precision, matching the group's strikes blow for blow. Kaelion's reflection fought with an eerie familiarity, every movement a perfect mirror of his own.

"They're us," Liora shouted, her blade clashing against her own reflection's. "Every move we make—they match it!"

"They're not us," Tavriel said, his staff glowing as he deflected an attack from his own reflection. "They're the Axis's judgment—measuring our threads, testing our choices."

Kaelion pushed forward, his breath heavy as he fought his way toward the shard. His reflection blocked his path, its strikes unrelenting. Each clash of their blades sent ripples through the air, the shard's resonance growing louder with every moment.

Kaelion's movements slowed as the shard's resonance shifted, its energy pressing against him like an unrelenting tide. His reflection's strikes grew faster, more precise, forcing him back step by step.

"You carry the threads of what is broken," the reflection said, its voice sharp. "But what will you sever to make them whole?"

Kaelion gritted his teeth, his voice firm. "I've heard this before. And my answer hasn't changed."

The reflection lunged, its blade flashing with raw energy. Kaelion parried the strike, his movements deliberate as he countered with a powerful blow that sent his reflection staggering.

He seized the moment, pushing past the mirrored figure and toward the shard. The threads surrounding it lashed out, their movements chaotic and violent. Kaelion raised his hand, his fingers brushing against the shard's surface.

The world shifted.

Kaelion stood in the void once more, the shard's core glowing faintly before him. The threads surrounding it were tangled and frayed, their movements clashing and unraveling in chaotic bursts.

A voice echoed through the void, calm and resonant. "The loom breaks. The threads fray. What will you weave to make it whole?"

Kaelion's chest tightened as the threads began to weave into shapes. Memories flickered before him—Selara's laughter, Darith's loss,

Tavriel's quiet wisdom, Liora's resilience. Each memory was a thread, fragile and fleeting, waiting to be woven into the loom.

"I'll weave what's needed," Kaelion said quietly, his voice steady. "But I won't do it alone."

The threads surged toward him, their energy pressing against him like a storm. Kaelion moved with purpose, his strikes deliberate as he severed the broken threads and wove the stable ones into place.

The shard's resonance shifted, its chaotic hum softening into a steady rhythm. The void stilled, the threads weaving together into intricate patterns that flickered with the promise of unity.

Kaelion opened his eyes to the battlefield, the shard standing before him. Its surface was smooth and reflective now, its light glowing with a quiet strength.

The mirrored figures surrounding them dissolved into threads of light and shadow, their energy spiraling back toward the shard's core. The air grew still, the shard's resonance fading into a quiet hum.

Tavriel approached cautiously, his staff glowing faintly. "The threads are holding. The loom remains intact—for now."

Kaelion nodded, his chest heaving as he lowered his sword. "But the loom isn't finished yet."

Liora stepped forward, her expression weary but resolute. "We're running out of time. The threads are fraying faster than we can weave them."

Kaelion's gaze turned toward the horizon, where the faint glow of the next shard shimmered in the distance.

"Then we keep moving. We finish this."

# Chapter Twenty-Nine: The Axis's Edge

The ground gave way beneath them. One moment, the group stood on the crystalline surface of the shattered loom, the horizon streaked with light and shadow. The next, they were falling into darkness, their surroundings shifting and blurring as if the very fabric of the world had turned to liquid.

Kaelion hit solid ground with a sharp thud, his breath forced from his lungs. Around him, faint glimmers of light pulsed, illuminating the faces of his companions as they picked themselves up from the endless void.

"What... just happened?" Darith asked, his voice uncharacteristically shaken.

Tavriel steadied himself with his staff, his blind eyes glimmering faintly. "The loom's core. We're no longer on its edges. We've fallen into its heart."

The air around them was thick and humming, alive with energy that pressed against their senses. The void was not empty—threads of light and shadow wove themselves into shifting patterns, forming spirals and lattices that flickered in and out of existence.

Kaelion pushed himself upright, his gaze scanning the endless void. "Where's the shard?"

Tavriel pointed ahead, where a single, blinding light burned at the center of the shifting patterns. The shard floated in the void, its surface glowing with raw, unrestrained energy.

"That's not a shard," Tavriel said softly. "That's the Axis's essence."

Kaelion took a cautious step forward, the ground beneath him rippling with his movement. The shard's resonance was deafening, a constant hum that vibrated through his bones.

"This is it," he said, his voice steady despite the chaos around him. "The final shard."

Liora stepped beside him, her blade drawn. "It doesn't look like it's going to come quietly."

As if in response, the threads surrounding the shard began to unravel, their movements erratic and violent. Figures emerged from the chaos, their forms jagged and indistinct. Unlike the previous reflections, these figures were incomplete—half-formed constructs of light and shadow, their movements sharp and unpredictable.

"They're fractures," Tavriel said, his voice tense. "Pieces of the Axis's will, broken and twisted by its collapse."

Kaelion drew his sword, his grip tightening. "Then we finish what we started."

The figures attacked with a ferocity unlike anything they had faced before. Kaelion met the first wave head-on, his strikes cutting through their forms with bursts of radiant energy. Each blow sent ripples through the void, the shard's resonance growing louder with every moment.

Darith moved with precision, his blade flashing as he struck down one of the figures. "They're faster than the others. Stronger, too."

"They're part of the Axis," Tavriel said, his staff glowing faintly as he chanted a low incantation. "They're defending it from us—just as much as they're testing us."

Kaelion pushed forward, his breath heavy as he fought his way toward the shard. The figures pressed closer, their attacks relentless. The energy radiating from the shard burned against his skin, each step forward feeling like a battle in itself.

As Kaelion neared the shard, a new figure emerged from the chaos. It was taller than the others, its form more defined. It moved with a deliberate grace, its presence radiating power and authority.

Kaelion stopped, his chest tightening as the figure stepped forward. Its features were eerily familiar—an exact reflection of him, but with eyes that burned with an intensity that mirrored the shard's light.

"You weave to mend," the reflection said, its voice calm but sharp. "But what will you sever to finish the loom?"

Kaelion raised his sword, his voice steady. "I'll sever what I must. But I won't lose myself."

The reflection smiled faintly. "We shall see."

The battle against the reflection was unlike anything Kaelion had faced before. Every strike he made was countered with equal precision, every movement mirrored with unrelenting accuracy. The reflection fought not just with skill but with the same intentions Kaelion carried—each strike, each parry a challenge to his resolve.

Liora and Darith fought off the other constructs, their blades flashing in the dim light. Tavriel stood at the edge of the fray, his staff glowing as he guided the threads surrounding the shard, weaving them into a barrier to contain the chaos.

Kaelion's breath came in ragged gasps as he clashed with the reflection, their blades sparking with each impact. His grip tightened on his sword, his movements deliberate.

"You can't win," the reflection said, its tone calm. "You fight against yourself. Against your own doubts, your own fears. Until you sever them, you cannot complete the loom."

Kaelion's jaw tightened. "I don't need to win. I just need to weave."

With a powerful strike, Kaelion forced the reflection back, its form flickering like a dying flame. He seized the moment, pushing past it and toward the shard. The threads surrounding it lashed out violently, their movements erratic and unpredictable.

He raised his hand, his fingers brushing against the shard's surface.

The world shifted.

Kaelion stood in the void, the shard's core glowing brightly before him. The threads surrounding it were tangled and frayed, their movements clashing and unraveling in chaotic bursts.

A voice echoed through the void, calm and resonant. "The loom waits. The Axis calls. What will you weave to bring it together?"

Kaelion's chest tightened as the threads began to weave into shapes. Memories flickered before him—Selara's laughter, the faces of those he had saved and failed, the glimmers of light and shadow that had defined his journey.

"I'll weave what's needed," Kaelion said quietly, his voice steady. "But I'll do it on my terms."

The threads surged toward him, their energy pressing against him like a storm. Kaelion moved with purpose, his strikes deliberate as he severed the broken threads and wove the stable ones into place.

The shard's resonance shifted, its chaotic hum softening into a steady rhythm. The void stilled, the threads weaving together into intricate patterns that flickered with the promise of unity.

Kaelion opened his eyes to the battlefield, the shard standing before him. Its surface was smooth and reflective now, its light glowing with a quiet strength.

The constructs surrounding them dissolved into threads of light and shadow, their energy spiraling back toward the shard's core. The air grew still, the shard's resonance fading into a quiet hum.

Tavriel approached cautiously, his staff glowing faintly. "The Axis is waiting. This was its final test."

Kaelion nodded, his chest heaving as he lowered his sword. "Then let's finish it."

Liora stepped forward, her expression resolute. "The loom's core is next. No more shards, no more trials. Just the end."

Kaelion's gaze turned toward the faint light at the heart of the void.

"And the beginning," he said softly.

# Chapter Thirty: The Core's Call

The faint light ahead grew brighter with each step, until the group stood before the loom's heart. The core was vast and unending, a swirling mass of light and shadow entwined in a chaotic dance. Threads stretched outward from its center, weaving into patterns too intricate to follow.

The ground beneath them was no longer solid, but a translucent surface of shifting hues that pulsed with the core's resonance. The air was thick with energy, each breath a struggle against the weight of the Axis's presence.

Kaelion tightened his grip on his sword, his gaze fixed on the swirling core. "This is it," he said, his voice steady. "The loom's heart."

Tavriel stepped forward, his staff glowing faintly. "The threads here are alive. Every movement we make will ripple through the weave."

Darith glanced around, his hand resting on his hilt. "And if we make the wrong move?"

Tavriel's blind eyes narrowed. "Then the loom collapses. And everything goes with it."

The group moved cautiously, the translucent ground beneath their feet rippling with every step. The core's resonance grew louder, its vibrations pressing against their senses like an unrelenting tide.

Kaelion stopped a few paces from the core's edge, his chest tightening as he studied the swirling threads. Unlike the shards, the core's energy felt overwhelming—not raw or chaotic, but infinite.

"It's waiting for us," Liora said softly, her voice edged with unease.

"No," Tavriel said, his tone solemn. "It's watching us."

The core pulsed, and the threads surrounding it began to move. They spiraled outward in deliberate patterns, forming shapes that flickered with an eerie familiarity. Figures emerged from the shifting light and shadow—figures the group recognized immediately.

Selara stepped forward, her violet eyes glimmering with quiet sorrow. Behind her, the faces of Kaelion's fallen comrades flickered into being, their gazes steady but haunting.

Kaelion's breath caught in his chest. "These aren't echoes."

"They're fragments," Tavriel said, his voice tense. "Pieces of the loom's memory—woven from us, for us."

Selara's voice was soft but clear. "The loom remembers what you've lost. What you've sacrificed. But memory alone is not enough to weave it whole."

Kaelion stepped forward, his jaw tightening. "What do you want from us?"

The core pulsed, and Selara's gaze met his. "The loom waits. The Axis calls. But you must choose what to leave behind—and what to carry forward."

The threads surrounding the core began to unravel, their movements slow and deliberate. The figures stepped forward, their forms flickering like flames.

Kaelion's grip on his sword tightened. "These aren't just memories. They're challenges."

Tavriel nodded, his expression grim. "The Axis is testing us. Every choice we've made, every thread we've woven—it's all leading here."

Liora drew her blade, her voice steady. "Then we fight. Together."

The battle erupted with a sudden ferocity. The figures moved with a fluid grace, their strikes precise and unrelenting. Kaelion met Selara's form head-on, his strikes cutting through her with bursts of radiant energy. Each blow sent ripples through the void, the core's resonance growing louder with every moment.

Darith fought beside him, his movements quick and deliberate. "These things are stronger than anything we've faced before."

"They're part of the core," Tavriel called out, his staff glowing faintly as he deflected another attack. "They're tied to the Axis itself."

Kaelion pushed forward, his breath heavy as he fought his way toward the core. Selara's form blocked his path, her strikes matching his own with unrelenting precision.

"You weave to mend," she said, her voice calm. "But what will you sever to make the loom whole?"

Kaelion's chest tightened as her blade struck against his, the impact sending a shockwave through the void.

"I'll sever what I must," he said firmly. "But I won't lose myself."

With a powerful strike, Kaelion forced Selara's form back, her image flickering like a dying flame. He seized the moment, pushing past her and toward the core. The threads surrounding it lashed out violently, their movements erratic and unpredictable.

He raised his hand, his fingers brushing against the core's surface.

The world shifted.

Kaelion stood in a void of pure light and shadow, the core's heart glowing brightly before him. The threads surrounding it were tangled and frayed, their movements clashing and unraveling in chaotic bursts.

A voice echoed through the void, calm and resonant. "The Axis calls. The loom waits. What will you weave to bind it together?"

Kaelion's breath steadied as he reached out, his hand brushing against the threads. Memories surged through him—Selara's laughter, Tavriel's wisdom, Liora's resilience, Darith's loyalty. Each memory was a thread, fragile and fleeting, waiting to be woven into the loom.

"I'll weave what's needed," Kaelion said quietly. "But I won't do it alone."

The threads surged toward him, their energy pressing against him like a storm. Kaelion moved with purpose, his strikes deliberate as he severed the broken threads and wove the stable ones into place.

The core's resonance shifted, its chaotic hum softening into a steady rhythm. The void stilled, the threads weaving together into intricate patterns that flickered with the promise of unity.

Kaelion opened his eyes to the battlefield, the core standing before him. Its surface was smooth and reflective now, its light glowing with a quiet strength.

The figures surrounding them dissolved into threads of light and shadow, their energy spiraling back toward the core. The air grew still, the core's resonance fading into a quiet hum.

Tavriel approached cautiously, his staff glowing faintly. "The loom is almost whole. The final thread is yours to weave, Kaelion."

Kaelion nodded, his chest heaving as he lowered his sword. "Then let's finish this."

The core pulsed one last time, its light growing brighter as it awaited their final choice.

# Chapter Thirty-One: Threads of Sacrifice

The core pulsed with a steady, resonant light, casting shifting patterns of shadow and illumination across the translucent ground. Around Kaelion and his companions, the figures of memory had dissolved into spiraling threads, their energy retreating into the loom's swirling heart. The air was still now, but it carried a sense of expectancy, as if the Axis itself awaited their next move.

"This is the end, isn't it?" Darith asked, his voice low but steady.

"No," Tavriel said softly, his blind gaze fixed on the glowing core. "This is the beginning of something entirely new. But only if we weave it right."

Kaelion stepped forward, his sword lowered but still in hand. The threads surrounding the core seemed to reach for him, their movements slow and deliberate. "What do we need to do?"

Tavriel's expression was solemn. "The final weave requires a thread from each of us—a piece of ourselves to bind the loom together."

"What kind of thread?" Liora asked, her tone sharp with suspicion.

"The deepest kind," Tavriel said, his voice barely above a whisper. "Memory. Hope. Fear. What we surrender to the loom will shape the new Axis."

Kaelion's chest tightened as he stared at the core, its surface glowing with a quiet, steady light. Memories surged through him unbidden—the faces of those he had failed to save, the laughter of comrades long gone, the haunting image of Selara's violet eyes filled with quiet sorrow.

"If we give a piece of ourselves to the loom," Kaelion said, his voice measured, "what happens to us?"

Tavriel turned toward him, his expression unreadable. "We lose what we give. Forever."

Liora frowned, her grip tightening on her blade. "You're saying we have to sacrifice part of who we are to fix this thing?"

"Not just fix it," Tavriel said. "Reforge it. The Axis will be reborn from what we choose to surrender. It will carry the essence of our sacrifices into the new weave."

Darith crossed his arms, his gaze hard. "And if we don't?"

Tavriel's staff glimmered faintly in the core's light. "The loom collapses. The world ends."

Silence fell over the group, the weight of Tavriel's words pressing against them. Kaelion's grip on his sword tightened, his gaze fixed on the core. The threads surrounding it pulsed softly, their movements deliberate but patient.

"I'll go first," Kaelion said, his voice steady.

Liora stepped forward sharply. "Wait! Shouldn't we—"

"No," Kaelion interrupted, his tone firm. "This started with me. I won't ask anyone to give more than I'm willing to."

He approached the core, the ground beneath his feet rippling with each step. The threads surrounding it reached for him, their movements slow and deliberate. Kaelion stopped a pace from the core, his chest tightening as he raised his hand.

The threads coiled around his arm, their touch cool and strangely gentle. The core pulsed, its light growing brighter as Kaelion closed his eyes.

Memories surged through him in vivid detail. He was back in Solaris, standing before a field of fallen villagers, their faces pale in the golden light. The weight of his guilt pressed against him, sharp and unrelenting.

"I failed them," Kaelion whispered, his voice breaking. "I couldn't save them."

A voice echoed softly, calm and resonant. "What will you weave from your failure?"

Kaelion opened his eyes, his breath steady. "Redemption. Hope. I'll weave the strength to carry on, even when I falter."

The core pulsed, and a thread of radiant light unraveled from Kaelion's chest. It glimmered faintly as it spiraled into the loom, weaving itself into the intricate patterns surrounding the core.

Kaelion staggered back, his chest heaving as the threads released him. A faint sense of emptiness lingered in his chest, but it was accompanied by a quiet resolve.

Liora stepped forward next, her blade sheathed but her posture rigid. The threads reached for her as she approached, their movements hesitant.

"What will you weave?" the voice asked softly.

Liora's jaw tightened. "Strength. But not for me. For the people I couldn't protect."

The threads coiled around her, their touch drawing a thread of shadowlight from her core. It shimmered faintly as it wove into the loom, joining Kaelion's thread in its delicate patterns.

She stepped back, her expression weary but resolute.

Darith followed, his movements uncharacteristically subdued. The threads wrapped around him, their touch coaxing a faint thread of golden light from his chest.

"I'll weave loyalty," he said quietly. "For the ones who stood beside me. For the ones who didn't make it."

Tavriel was last. The threads surrounding the core seemed to hesitate as he stepped forward, their movements slow and deliberate.

"What will you weave?" the voice asked.

Tavriel's blind eyes glimmered faintly, his expression unreadable. "Wisdom," he said softly. "And memory. Even if it's not mine to keep."

The threads unraveled a delicate thread of shimmering light from his chest, weaving it into the loom with the others.

The core pulsed brighter as the final threads wove into place, its resonance shifting into a steady, harmonious rhythm. The void around them began to ripple and change, the translucent ground beneath their feet solidifying into something brighter, more vivid.

Kaelion stepped back, his chest heaving as the core's light grew blinding. "It's done," he said quietly. "The loom is whole."

The core pulsed once more, its light washing over them in a wave of warmth. The world shifted, the void dissolving into a kaleidoscope of light and shadow.

When the light faded, they stood on solid ground again, the horizon stretching endlessly in every direction. The loom's threads shimmered faintly above them, weaving intricate patterns into the fabric of the world.

Tavriel's voice was soft. "The Axis is reborn. The weave is restored."

Kaelion's gaze turned toward the horizon, where faint streaks of light and shadow blended seamlessly into one another. "Then it's time to see what we've made."

# Chapter Thirty-Two: The Loom Reforged

The world was different.

Kaelion stood on solid ground, but it no longer felt like the fractured expanse of the shattered loom. The air shimmered faintly, alive with energy that hummed in harmony. The sky above them was a vast canvas, blending gradients of light and shadow in patterns that seemed to breathe.

The group stood in silence, their gazes fixed on the Axis. The core floated before them, its surface smooth and reflective, glowing with a quiet, steady light. Threads of radiant energy stretched outward from its center, weaving into the fabric of the world.

"It's done," Tavriel said softly, his voice laced with awe. "The loom is whole again."

Kaelion stepped forward, his gaze fixed on the Axis. Its light pulsed gently, and as he stared into its surface, his own reflection gazed back at him—steady and unbroken.

"What happens now?" Darith asked, his tone hesitant.

Tavriel turned toward him, his blind eyes glimmering faintly. "The Axis waits. The threads are mended, but the weave is incomplete. It's waiting for us to decide what comes next."

The ground beneath them rippled faintly, and the Axis pulsed brighter. Threads of light and shadow spiraled outward, weaving themselves into forms that flickered with familiarity.

Kaelion's breath caught as the figures of Selara, Laryn, and others they had lost appeared before them. Their faces were serene, their gazes steady.

"They're not real," Liora said softly, her voice trembling.

"No," Tavriel said. "They're memories. Threads from the loom itself, reflecting what we've given to it."

Selara stepped forward, her violet eyes filled with quiet sorrow. "The Axis is whole, but it's not yet woven. What will you make of it?"

Kaelion's grip on his sword tightened as he stepped toward her. "You're asking us to decide the fate of the world?"

Selara's smile was faint but warm. "You've already decided. Now, you must weave it."

The threads spiraled around them, their movements deliberate and patient. The figures faded into the shimmering fabric of the loom, leaving the group standing alone before the Axis.

Kaelion turned toward Tavriel. "What do we do?"

Tavriel's blind gaze fixed on the Axis, his expression unreadable. "We weave what we've learned. Light and shadow. Loss and hope. The threads we've given are the foundation. The rest is up to us."

Kaelion stepped closer to the Axis, his chest tightening as its resonance pressed against him. Memories surged through him—of battles fought and lost, of choices made and regrets carried.

"We weave balance," he said quietly. "Not perfection. Not control. Just balance."

The Axis pulsed brighter as Kaelion raised his hand, his fingers brushing against its surface. The threads surrounding it surged forward, coiling around his arm and pulling him into the core's light.

The world shifted.

Kaelion stood in the void once more, the Axis's heart glowing brightly before him. The threads surrounding it were alive, their movements weaving intricate patterns that flickered with potential.

A voice echoed softly, calm and resonant. "The loom waits. The threads are ready. Will you weave them?"

Kaelion's breath steadied as he reached out, his hand brushing against the threads. Memories surged through him—Selara's laughter, Darith's loyalty, Liora's resilience, Tavriel's quiet wisdom. Each thread was a choice, fragile and fleeting, waiting to be woven into the loom.

"I'll weave what's needed," Kaelion said softly. "But I won't do it alone."

The threads surged toward him, their energy pressing against him like a storm. Kaelion moved with purpose, his strikes deliberate as he severed the broken threads and wove the stable ones into place. Each movement was careful, each choice deliberate.

As he worked, the void around him began to change. The swirling patterns of light and shadow grew steadier, their movements synchronizing into a harmonious rhythm. The Axis's light pulsed brighter, its resonance shifting into a steady, melodic hum.

Kaelion opened his eyes to the battlefield, the Axis standing before him. Its surface was smooth and reflective, its light glowing with a quiet strength.

The world around them was whole. The fractured landscape of the loom had been replaced with something vibrant and alive—a realm where light and shadow blended seamlessly, their contrasts enhancing one another.

Tavriel stepped forward, his blind gaze fixed on the Axis. "The weave is complete. The world has been remade."

Kaelion nodded, his chest heaving with the weight of what they had accomplished. "But at what cost?"

Liora placed a hand on his shoulder, her expression resolute. "We gave what we had to. And we've gained something worth it."

The group stood in silence, their gazes fixed on the horizon. The threads of the loom shimmered faintly above them, weaving into patterns that stretched endlessly into the distance.

Kaelion's voice was soft but steady. "This isn't the end. It's the start of something new."

Tavriel's smile was faint but knowing. "The weave is never finished, Kaelion. It continues with every choice, every step forward."

The Axis pulsed softly, its light fading into the background as the group turned toward the horizon.

Kaelion's hand rested on the hilt of his sword as he took the first step forward, his gaze fixed on the endless expanse ahead.

"Let's see what we've made."

# Chapter Thirty-Three: The Eclipse Eternal

The horizon was endless.

Kaelion led the group across the new world's unmarred expanse, where light and shadow no longer clashed but flowed together in seamless harmony. The sky above them shimmered like a living tapestry, threads of radiant energy weaving intricate patterns that shifted and danced with their every step. The air carried a faint hum, not oppressive, but soothing—an echo of the Axis's steady pulse.

"This place..." Darith's voice was hushed, almost reverent. "It feels alive. Like it's breathing with us."

"It is," Tavriel said softly. "The loom isn't just the world's foundation—it's part of it. Part of us."

Kaelion glanced back at his companions, his grip on his sword loose but instinctive. The weight of their journey still pressed on him, but the world around them seemed to lighten it with every step.

"It's strange," Liora said, her tone contemplative. "After everything we gave up, I don't feel empty. I feel... full. Like the piece I lost is still here, just in a different way."

"It is," Tavriel replied. "The loom doesn't take—it transforms. What we surrendered is woven into the world. It's why the Axis shines brighter now. It carries us forward."

The group stopped at the edge of a vast cliff, its surface smooth and reflective like polished obsidian. Below, a great sea stretched out into the distance, its waves shimmering with light and shadow entwined. Kaelion stepped closer to the edge, the wind brushing against his face as he gazed at the horizon.

The sea mirrored his reflection, but it wasn't just him. The faces of those he had lost shimmered faintly in the water's surface—Selara, Laryn, and countless others whose threads had shaped his journey.

"They're still here," Kaelion said quietly.

"They always will be," Tavriel said, stepping to his side. "The loom remembers. The threads of those we've lost are part of its weave now."

Kaelion's chest tightened, but not with sorrow. It was a quiet, steady resolve—a sense that his losses, his sacrifices, had meaning beyond the pain they had caused.

The Axis shimmered faintly behind them, its light dimming as the group moved further from its core. Kaelion turned toward Tavriel, his brow furrowing. "What happens to the Axis now? Does it just... fade away?"

Tavriel shook his head. "The Axis doesn't fade. It doesn't end. It watches, it waits, and it weaves. Its work is never truly done."

Darith chuckled softly, his tone light but tinged with weariness. "Sounds a lot like us, doesn't it?"

Liora smiled faintly, her hand resting on the hilt of her blade. "I think we've earned a little rest, though. Don't you?"

Kaelion's gaze turned back to the horizon, his grip tightening slightly on his sword. "Rest can wait. The loom might be whole, but the world isn't. Not yet."

The group descended from the cliff, their steps purposeful but unhurried. The path before them was unmarked, the terrain shifting and forming as they moved forward. The threads of the loom shimmered faintly in the air, weaving patterns that seemed to guide their way.

Tavriel slowed his pace, his staff tapping lightly against the ground. "This is the nature of the weave. It doesn't dictate—it offers possibilities. Every step we take shapes it, every choice we make strengthens it."

Kaelion nodded, his expression contemplative. "Then we make it count."

The group stopped at a crossroads, where the land split into three distinct paths. One was bathed in soft, golden light, its surface smooth and inviting. Another was cloaked in shadow, its path winding and uncertain. The third shimmered faintly, its boundaries blurred and shifting like water.

Kaelion looked to his companions, his gaze steady. "We choose together."

Liora stepped forward, her expression resolute. "The light's path is clear, but too easy. That's not how we got here."

Darith nodded. "The shadow's tempting. It offers strength, but it's strength without purpose."

Tavriel raised his staff, gesturing toward the shifting path. "The third path is the weave itself. Uncertain. Unfinished. But full of potential."

Kaelion stepped toward the third path, his voice firm. "Then that's the one we take."

The group moved forward, the path shifting beneath their feet. The air grew warmer, the hum of the loom growing fainter as the Axis receded into the distance. Kaelion felt a quiet resolve settle over him, the weight of their journey giving way to the promise of what lay ahead.

As they walked, the threads of the loom shimmered faintly above them, weaving into patterns that stretched endlessly into the distance.

Kaelion's voice was soft but steady. "This isn't the end."

"No," Tavriel said with a faint smile. "It's just the beginning."

The group moved forward together, their steps purposeful and united, as the new world unfolded around them.

EPILOGUE: THREADS UNBROKEN

The air was quiet, carrying the faint scent of dew and earth. On the horizon, the sun hovered low, its golden light blending seamlessly with the deepening shadows of the approaching night. In this new world, twilight had no fixed place—it lingered, a testament to the unity that now bound light and shadow.

Kaelion stood atop a hill, his gaze sweeping over the land below. Fields of silver-green grass rippled like water in the wind, their edges shimmering with faint traces of light and shadow entwined. Villages dotted the landscape, their humble buildings aglow with a warm luminescence that seemed to rise from the earth itself.

A quiet peace had settled over the land, but Kaelion knew it was fragile. The loom's threads were whole, but they were still young—untested, like the people now tasked with weaving a future from them.

Footsteps crunched softly behind him.

"You're not much for resting, are you?" Liora's voice carried a note of amusement as she stepped beside him.

Kaelion smiled faintly, his hand resting lightly on the hilt of his sword. "The world doesn't stop moving just because we've finished our part."

She followed his gaze, her expression thoughtful. "We've done more than our part, Kaelion. We've given this world a chance to rebuild. That's enough."

"Maybe for us," he said, his tone soft but steady. "But not for them." He nodded toward the distant village, where faint trails of smoke curled into the twilight sky. "The people down there—they don't know what this world cost. What it took to make it whole again. All they'll see is what's in front of them. And that's exactly how it should be."

Liora studied him for a moment, her gaze searching. "You're not staying, are you?"

Kaelion's smile was faint, but it carried a quiet sadness. "I've never been good at staying."

Down the hill, Darith was lighting a fire outside a modest wooden cabin. The glow of the flames reflected in his features, softening the lines of weariness etched into his face.

Nearby, Tavriel sat cross-legged, his staff resting beside him. His blind eyes were closed, his expression serene. The faint hum of the loom was barely audible in the air around him, a constant reminder of the threads that bound them all.

"They'll be fine," Liora said, her voice quiet.

"I know," Kaelion replied. He watched as Darith waved Tavriel over, the two of them exchanging words too soft to hear. The firelight caught in Tavriel's silver-threaded hair, making it glow faintly in the deepening dusk.

"They've earned their rest," Kaelion added. "And so have you."

"What about you?" Liora asked, her tone pointed.

Kaelion turned to her, his gaze steady. "I'll rest when I'm finished."

The two of them descended the hill together, the wind brushing softly against their faces. As they reached the cabin, Darith grinned and gestured toward the fire.

"Thought you'd never come down," he said, tossing another log onto the flames. "Figured you'd decided to keep brooding up there all night."

Kaelion chuckled, the sound quiet but genuine. "Just taking in the view."

Tavriel opened his eyes, his blind gaze turning toward Kaelion. "The view may change, but the threads remain constant. You'll see them wherever you go."

Kaelion nodded, his smile faint. "I know."

The fire crackled softly as the group sat together, the twilight deepening around them. For a moment, there was nothing but the warmth of the flames, the murmur of the wind, and the faint hum of the loom.

Kaelion leaned back, his gaze fixed on the horizon. In his mind, the threads of the world stretched endlessly, each one carrying the promise of a choice yet to be made.

"This isn't the end," he said softly, almost to himself.

"No," Tavriel replied, his voice steady. "It's just another thread in the weave."

As the stars began to emerge, their light blending with the soft glow of the horizon, Kaelion rose. His companions watched him in silence, their expressions understanding.

"Where will you go?" Liora asked.

Kaelion's smile was faint but resolute. "Wherever the threads lead me."

He clasped hands with each of them in turn, his grip firm and steady. Then, without another word, he turned and began to walk into the twilight, his silhouette blending with the shifting light and shadow of the new world.

The others watched him go until the horizon swallowed him, the soft hum of the loom their only companion.

And in the distance, Kaelion walked onward, one step at a time, carrying the weight of the threads—and the promise of a new world—with him.

The End of The Eclipse Chronicles

# Also by Kenneth Thomas

**The Awakening Thread Chronicles**
The Awakening Thread

**The Convergence of Minds series**
The Digital Agora: A Philosophical Epic of AI and Humanity
Foundation of the Agora
Beyond the Agora: Fractured Realms

**The Eclipse Chronicles**
Shards of Light
Eclipse Reaver
Axis Reforged

**The Veil of Shadows Series**
Shattered Dominion
The Fractured Path